I0684509

SCHOOL OF THE WOLVEN WAY

BY NEVELIOUS JORDAN

ISBN-13: 9780692961766
ISBN-10: 0692961763

Shatteringham Books
P.O. Box 2934
Washington D.C. 20013
10 9 8 7 6 5 4 3 2 1

For Jermayne Wright, who now rests without pain.

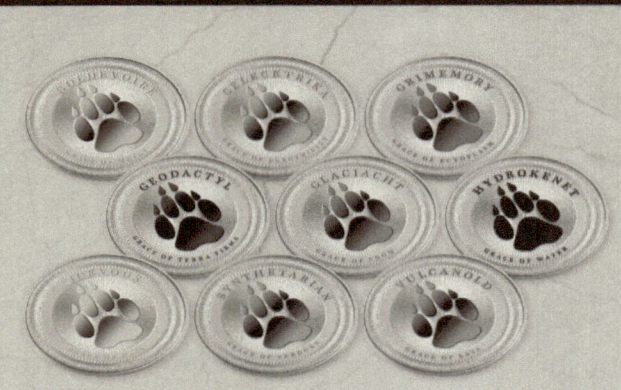

Sight heightened Earth's metaphysical consciousness long before the planet was overpopulated. With it, the elements saw their reflection and the eventual creation of man. They soon witnessed the barbarism and greed that humans are capable of, watching themselves be polluted and commodified.

To preserve their sanctity, they split their consciousnesses. Half created the Celortus, beings that allowed them to speak and feel emotions. The other half created their protectors, who draw their might from elemental empowerment.

These are the graced children. They are the Elehominum.

Bennington Court of Cumberchester Heights, 1925

CHAPTER I

Students within the District of Columbia Public School system always eagerly awaited the last day of the instructional year. It was an interlude of celebration, one where the endless possibilities of summer came alive. The constant fear of being stuffed inside cramped lockers was erased from each previous victim's mind, no different than how the multicolored hopscotch squares were wiped clean from the blacktops. Gut-wrenching anxieties of being retained in one's current level due to failing standardized tests were eased.

Those all-too-common worries were replaced with strolls through the outlet shopping malls of western Maryland, water gun battles at pricey amusement parks in northern Virginia, and the freedom of being unsupervised by parents who could not afford to take off from work to ensure there was no mischief brewing. The normal ones had it easy. Julien Preux had not been fortunate enough to count himself among them.

The sixth period bell rang and children from Frederick Douglass Junior High poured out of four available exits the red-bricked building had to offer. Their rapid movements mimicked the commotion of starved herds feeding. As they trampled one another, conversations that centered around acts of immature debauchery, like sneaking into R-rated movies and egging the strictest administrators' cars, were held at the loudest volume.

Julien, carried out into the sunlit June afternoon by polished Kenneth Cole dress shoes, preferred to scan his report card rather than participate in juvenile matters. His final grades were perfect with the exception of French, a language that he should have been far better at mastering, considering the fact that he was a second-generation Haitian-American on both sides.

"C+ again? That's seriously two whole advisories I've gotten the same score. I revise my lessons every fricking night and still can't improve. I should have just taken Spanish," the overachieving boy grumbled, folding the sheet that tracked his progress and placing it in the back pocket of the khaki pants he wore.

Gripping the reinforced straps of his backpack, Julien walked past the Kesher Israel Congregation synagogue, a staple in his Georgetown neighborhood. Part of the only black family in the area, he was easily distinguishable from its snobby Caucasian residents. It did not hurt that his father, Charles, was the local urologist, either. Most were nice enough, but there were a handful who did not care how much money the Preux family bankrolled; they did not want *them* for neighbors.

Mrs. Lebowitz was one of those types. She was a stubby Jewish woman, with bushy white hair and a hairy mole on her right cheek. A widow with no children, the senior citizen spent her days sitting on the porch, chain-smoking Marlboro cigarettes. When one of the Preuxs tried to greet her, she simply looked away. Waving at her, Julien was not offended by the old bat ignoring him. If her lungs ever collapsed, he would return the favor. Shrugging, he leaned in to unlock the door with the key that was attached to his Gucci belt and entered.

Georgetown homes were inherently lavish, but it was the interior decoration that made the Preux household unique. Paintings designed by famed Pakistani artist Ustad Allah Bux hung on the first-floor walls. Light shined through imported Sicilian drapes. From the kitchen, Julien's mother, Sandra, sang along to the rhythmic sounds of Caribbean reggae musicians. Born to lovers of exploration, he was exposed to numerous cultures the day he left the womb. Knowing the chronological order of Canada's prime ministers, reciting the Greek alphabet, and counting to ten in Estonian were among the skills he picked up on their annual vacations abroad. Recently, he had grown interested in the country in which his great-grandfather died.

Jean-Renee Preux was not a name that would be in any bibliography or directory. He was Haiti's first and only successful alchemist, or so the Preux family myths claimed. Formerly passed down from generation to generation was a story that described his discovery of how to transmutate cinnabarite into gold. He became rich by selling the fruits of his labor to traveling jewelers who, in turn, told their associates about "the man who could weave treasure from scratch."

His money was then extended to his brothers and sons. He retired to Tyne and Wear, a metropolitan county in the north east region of England, and his final days ended with the peace of mind that his bloodline would prosper. However, the older the goldsmith became, the less his tales of changing chemical properties seemed realistic. It was the evolving field of science that fueled disbelief. At his burial, most reasoned he was a mere drug dealer of a rare hallucinogenic.

The oldest Preux men decided to burn the scarce pictures of Jean-Renee and with them, the thought of owing their success to someone they saw as a common criminal. All that remained was a tin foil notepad of complex formulas that listed infinite mathematical algorithms. It, too, would have been destroyed had Julien not begged his father to keep it. He was entranced by the fine penmanship.

"Alchemy might sound cool, son, but we've come a long way since your great-grandfather was buried in that godforsaken Cumberchester Heights. You come from a line of medical trendsetters who really have made a difference in this world. Your grandfather practically did open heart surgeries with his eyes closed. I get urology awards monthly and my YouTube channel almost has a million subscribers. I think that gives you a reason to pursue a *real* science," Charles once said.

A career of examining body parts, especially male genitals, did not enthuse the youngest Preux but he knew his father. If he got one look at the stellar scores that his son received in biology, the bald-headed man would never shut up about career options. It was inevitable that his report card would be requested for viewing by his parents, but he dreaded that it would be tonight. The nagging had become annoying to say the least.

That was precisely why Julien crept to the top floor of the house. Stealthy slides led him across a vanilla rug and out of the hallway. He made it to his sanctuary of privacy, where twelve angelfishes confined to a 55-gallon tank swam. Slipping out of his shoes, he stretched.

Crumpled paper littered the otherwise spotless surface of Julien's spacious bedroom. They were the French exams that he had not passed. He mashed them with bare feet and scooped up one, the bulk of it carefully balanced on his big toe.

Slowly bringing his knee to his chest, Julien's eyes targeted the plastic trashcan that was positioned diagonally from him. Flicking his foot, he watched the makeshift ball travel. Bouncing off the wall, it landed inside and he scarcely avoided hitting his head on the ceiling lamp from jumping in joy. Reminiscing of two months prior, he wished his cousin could have seen what he did.

In the wake of April, Anedie, Julien's aunt from Port-au-Prince, arrived at the Ronald Reagan National Airport, temporarily seeking refuge because Hurricane Matthew had dismantled her residence. Her troublesome son, Emmanuel, flew in on a package deal, a detail that was conveniently unmentioned until an hour before the flight. The unfortunate surprise was the source of disgruntlement from Sandra. To Julien, his cousin was a coach who would never grow sick of his athletic shortcomings. To her, he was a bad influence that she wanted kept at an island's distance.

"We open our home to her and what happens?

Anedie finds a way to take advantage of our kindness. She knows I don't want that boy anywhere near us. It's just like her to be underhanded and conniving. I'm not the least bit surprised," Sandra often groaned.

Julien's mother was proud of her heritage. She felt that it was her duty to help her half-sister, but the accent that once coated her words in anger had faded and with it, according to Anedie, her ethnic identity. Had she been raised in the old country's villages, she might have been ashamed to be the recipient of such a nasty accusation. If excusing Emmanuel's poor behavior stripped her of the ancestry that tailored her genetics, though, she was decidedly whitewashed. Sandra refused to enable him.

The 18-year-old roughneck stood six feet tall and was a mountain of lean muscle, his body sculpted from years of competitive soccer in detention centers across Haiti. Peach fuzz pitifully grew in patches crosswise his sturdy chin, but dreadlocks went from his scalp to the end of his shoulder blades. Tattooed grenade launchers and grim reapers covered his forearms. Unlike the rest of his kin, he was coffee-complexioned and had the distinct feature of hazel eyes. His combination of appealing looks and bad boy swagger made girls fawn and boys nod with respect. Emmanuel was the epitome of Julien's antithesis: a handsome thief with a silver tongue.

While Emmanuel's five-finger discount tricks and teachings of Kreyòl vulgarities were explicitly prohibited by Julien's parents, he found no resistance in his offering to instruct his younger cousin on how to dribble and defend in soccer post-homework. Mr. and Mrs. Preux did what they could to prevent the air of delinquency from spreading to their son, but thought he deserved a chance to bond with his cousin.

After Julien's hand stung from the painstakingly slow writing that came with nightly chapter outlines of the reading for his advanced placement English class, he retraced the checklist of lingering assignments that were inked in the planner his school mandated for ninth graders. Like clockwork, he always managed to be done at sunset. That was when the boys would hurry to the backyard, where they were surrounded by lush grass that looked moist under moonlight.

A clay flower pot was tipped to serve as the goal. Until Mrs. Lebowitz routinely knocked on the door to complain about their activities keeping her awake, Emmanuel tried to mold a decent player out of a klutz. The shorter of the two fought to find coordination. He regularly tripped over his feet and fell face-first onto bustling anthills. No ridicule came from that lack of athleticism, only an explanation that confidence was necessary for any endeavor.

"Don't be scared to try, kouzen; that's how you learn."

Had Emmanuel been there to see the aforementioned impressive feat, pride would have overtaken him. It would have been the concrete evidence that proved to everyone he was not a full-on knucklehead. Beneath his grimy past was the power to motivate for positivity. Julien was in the process of sending him a WhatsApp text message, but Sandra interrupted him.

"Juju, your father had a stressful day at the office and was snoring on the couch, but he heard your feet slamming. We didn't even know you came in. What are you doing in here that's causing that ruckus?"

The chubby-cheeked woman that stood in the doorway was more cautious than angry. A famed metal sculptor with an appreciation of artistic expression in minors, she always said she would not forgive herself if she ever stifled creativity in him. Julien knew why. He was 15-years-old, the same age she was when she found the passion that garnered her global notoriety. She was infinitely less adamant about pressuring him to lay out his life's path than Charles.

"Sorry, Mom, I didn't think I was that loud. I got a little excited because I made the shot I thought I never would. It would've been great if Emmanuel saw it. I was actually just about to tell him."

"Before you do that, maybe you should take a look at something. The mailman delivered this for you today. It came from some school in England. You're just like your father and I; a young traveler in the making. I can't wait to hear what's in store for you over dinner!"

A manila envelope was pulled from its hiding place behind the back of her black and white striped t-shirt. Smiling, she sat it atop the dresser near his door and moved out of sight, light marching taking her back downstairs. Perplexed, Julien wondered what business a school in England had with him. He had not researched nor scheduled any campus tours. How his name and address were obtained by people that he never volunteered them to was worrisome. The deep web conspiracy blogs he frequented were dominated by warnings of the dangers associated with unsecured social media. A birthday and picture were liable to get an entire social security number stolen.

Impatience caused him to skip perusing the front and rush to overturn it so that he could dig under the sealed flap. Nervously, he shook out the contents. Inside was a crisp letter.

"Dear Mister Julien Michel Preux, it is with great admiration that Edenshire Academy, the leading collegiate preparatory school in Newcastle upon Tyne, seeks your enrollment in our annual summer enrichment program. This is a three-month-long intensive introduction to higher learning in the disciplines of astronomy, algebra, art, botany, foreign languages, forensics, and literature. As this is also an opportunity for Edenshire Academy to further establish itself as the undisputed tender to multinational academic minds, we are pleased to announce that your expenses, from airfare to tuition to room and board, will be waived with a full scholarship. If you are interested, please visit the link nearest the bottom of this post and follow the instructions. We anticipate your decision," it read.

The end of the correspondence brought a calm. Gone were the unsettling what ifs of a hijacked social security number or a breached savings account. The mysterious sender's message was legitimized by a professional format. In the upper left-hand corner, there was a letterhead that, in bold Old English font, featured the school's name and above it, its coat of arms: a shield with the helmet of a knight to the left of it and to the right, a quill pen. Below the URL was a signature closing, complete with an employee ID and email address. Julien thought it was a surefire way to contact the composer: a Ms. Tatyana Rusev.

Although Julien had no intention of pursuing any of the fields that were supported by Edenshire Academy, he did see the value in attending because it would let him wander the city in which Jean-Renee died. He had an undeniable urge to see where the man whose work he felt destined to continue rested, a truth that he would not dare reveal to his father. Eyes closed, he confronted that belief. Since the age of five, he dreamed of a nude ebony man inside an adobe, pouring liquids onto carvings of the formulas from the notepad he cherished. What the man did after touching the wax was hidden by a blackout, but gold bars twinkled in the shadows.

Those subconscious images inspired Julien to collect particulars about alchemy. He began Sundays at nine, waking to eat one of the homemade granola bars that his mother baked and rode the G6 bus to the Farragut East subway station. Libraries in a ten-mile radius were ransacked for books on early practitioners. With the swipe of a card, he was in possession of rented knowledge.

Heavier than encyclopedias, the tattered texts traced the origins of alchemy to ancient Egypt, but expounded solely upon the theories of European men. On the hollow pages of a three-ring binder, Julien summarized what he reviewed. He had gained a fundamental understanding: alchemy was the technique of changing one element to another. The ever-fattening diary of critical analyses was secured in the back of his closet. If an alchemical code existed in his dreams, he believed it was part of Jean-Renee's formulas. The uncertainty of what they solved was eerily intriguing to him.

"His tombstone probably has more clues. I mean, people do take stuff they don't want anyone else knowing with them to the grave. I bet he wanted to share his processes with our family but they started doubting him so, he made the choice to keep them to himself. Yeah, that's it. Instead of helping other people get famous, he wanted to keep gold weaving in our lineage. It was supposed to be a gift for us. Those weird dreams I have are his way of communicating with me. He wants me to find the answers to what no one else bothered with. I know that's what he wants!"

Julien thought his rationalization sounded less peculiar in his head than it did spoken aloud. It was questionable, but he had the intuition that his dreams were attempting to verify the talents of his great-grandfather. Redeeming the legacy of the man responsible for the flourishing of the Preux dynasty fell squarely on his bony shoulders. It was no coincidence that letter came in the mail; it was fate. He had to go to England.

Even affairs that were expertly arranged by the hands of destiny could be trumped by authoritative orders. Julien's parents were, for the most part, lenient. Aside from hounding him to have a solid plan for his future, Charles was an easygoing man. Sandra just wanted to see him happy. They were reasonable and prudent. What they were not was careless. Both were acquainted with NBC4 news, and headlines about crimes against children kept them on guard. They knew the same kind of bastards that preyed on unsuspecting kids in the United States were present elsewhere, even in England.

If he was going to convince them to allow him

to be on another continent for the remainder of summertime without their supervision, he required ammunition. He had to make Edenshire Academy sound synonymous with paradise.

Flopping onto the polka-dotted sheets of his bed's king-sized mattress, Julien grabbed his Toshiba Satellite laptop and accessed the website link to the school's application. A background with pictures from the previous summer was the homepage. The students were showcased in unconventional workshop exercises, like painting the Mona Lisa on their desks and constructing hamburger meat models of the solar system. Scattered around were prints of the instructors, many of whom were barefaced university graduates, and their personalized quotes regarding education. The one that stood out the most came from an androgynous male.

"Here, we encourage young minds to break away from the archaic chains that bind them. There isn't one of our students who is not remarkable and won't go on to trigger brilliance, far and wide!"

It echoed the goofy assertions of a quintessential magnet school. Parroting the staff's cheesy, rehearsed statements would not suffice. Their unorthodox approach to schooling, however, was a start. Julien's free-spirited mother would surely think that it was a worthwhile investment because of the eccentric artwork. His strong-willed father would be a harder sell. The only place he wanted to see hamburger meat was between sesame seed buns, topped with ketchup, mustard, dill pickles, and extra cheddar cheese.

Faked awe in astronomy or botany was necessary to butter up Charles. If he assumed his son was well on his way to becoming an astronaut or a biochemist, he would agree to anything. To appear well-informed, Julien surfed the databases for overviews. A glance at the programs was all that it took for him to piece together probable justification for their permission.

Selecting astronomy was a no-brainer. Potential adventures were easy to craft if spaceships and walking on Mars with Martians were in the conversation. The application asked for the essentials, specifically: allergies, country of citizenship, grade point average, passport digits, and a summary of the applicant's aspirations. He lost track of time, fabricating six paragraphs of fictitious occasions of realizing he wanted to be the next Neil Armstrong. After sending the email, he was called to eat dinner. It was time for an award-winning performance.

Rising from his position on the bed, Julien grasped the letter and stood to the height of five foot five, squishing it into his back pocket while exiting his bedroom. He paused, gripping the unsteady banister. He was not used to lying to his parents, and it dawned on him that it wouldn't be as easy as he expected. He felt being dishonest with the two people that loved him unconditionally was wrong. The burden of heavy falsehoods anchored him.

Stiffness constricting his Adam's apple would prevent a seamless act of falsification. Quivering hands loosening the top four buttons of a somewhat wrinkled white shirt, Julien pushed off the endmost step. Combined smells of lemon-grilled Atlantic salmon with garlic asparagus permeated. It was his favorite meal.

"Hey, Dad, I didn't mean to wake you from your nap. I was just goofing off upstairs and got carried away. It won't happen again," he apologized, dallying to the dining room.

"Don't sweat it, kiddo. I was having a nightmare about being pecked to death by exploding chickens," said Charles. "I should be thanking you for saving me from a heart attack."

His voice was mighty, words booming like detonated dynamite. Two hundred pounds with the posture of a veteran Marine, Julien thought the idea of a man his size being afraid of anything was implausible. He was the head of the Preux household and yet, a childhood memory of being chased on a Kentucky ranch by an agitated hen distressed him. It was humorous that he was so terrified of farm animals, but those grins faded when he mentioned the mail.

"So, your mother tells me that you got a delivery from England. Why don't you bring us up to speed on that?"

"I wanted to tear it open myself but you're not a little kid anymore," Sandra chimed in, setting wrapped cutlery in front of Charles.

Sandra's cooking was nothing shy of perfection. The Preux family's friends claimed dishes she prepared rivaled winners of competitions hosted by alumni of Le Cordon Bleu. Julien remembered her saying that she was an ex-stress eater, and that she used to engorge her insides with sugar and sodium to cope with her sculptures not selling. Her luck took a turn for the better circa 2003, and the excess pounds put on from stuffing her face with fudge cake pops and deviled eggs dropped. She transformed from a pudgy butterball into a slim woman with chiseled calves that were the products of midday jogs and heavy squats. She had retained her culinary prowess, albeit in a healthier fashion.

Mouth watering, Julien reached for the silverware on opposite ends of his plate. Tasting fresh fish and tangy vegetables would take the edge off of fibbing, he hoped.

"It came from this school in Newcastle upon Tyne. Edenshire Academy's the name of it. They want me to be part of their summer enrichment program. I scoped them out and I want to go. They even have a course in astronomy. I started reading up on NASA. I think I'd like to be an astronaut."

Charles rushed to swallow a large portion of the fillet that he chewed on with a swig of cranberry juice. He was happy that his consistent badgering paid off, but the wanton inclination to brag to Sandra about having the correct setup to foster Julien's maturity was subdued. Instead of gloating, he delved further.

"That's terrific news, Juju! I knew you'd make a name for yourself in a real science. I said it years ago. I remember you were pleading with me not to throw out that flimsy notepad. Look at you now, an astronaut in the making. Why didn't you tell me sooner you were liking astronomy? My receptionist has a daughter that's coordinating internships."

Swallowing the food in his mouth saved Julien from having to verbally defend alchemy. Emphasis on the word "real" stung then just as much as it did the first go-round. His blatant disrespect would make learning to utilize those formulas more satisfying. A game of charades was to be played in the meantime.

"I was waiting for the right opportunity, I guess," Julien said between bites. "I know that you've been busy with opening your new offices in Baltimore and Philly. I didn't want to be an inconvenience."

"Don't be ridiculous; you could never be a bother. Your mother and I will always prioritize for you. You just have to speak and we'll listen."

Pouty lips licked clean of diet Pepsi Max, Sandra nodded in approval. She eavesdropped on many of her clients throughout the years, horrified to hear about the dwindling conditions of their children's mental stability. Psychiatrists labeled the boys and girls with irregularities they never heard of, swearing pills would rectify the issues. The few instances she met them, they were so doped they hardly spoke. Having her son drugged into a shell of his former self was out of the question. Any problems he had were going to be handled by her and Charles.

"He's right, sweetheart. Nothing matters more to us than having a bond with you. Now, going back to this school business, how much is it going to cost? Your father writes so many checks, I have to monitor our finances on a weekly basis."

"Not a cent. They said they wanted more international students with high grade point averages and if I applied, I would get a full scholarship. It's only for June, July, and August so it probably isn't too much money for them to spend."

Simultaneously, his parents stopped chewing. Neither of them could believe what they were hearing. It reeked of scam. Julien was very intelligent, neither of them denied that, but they pondered how a school in England found their son out of the trillion other brilliant minds in the United States. There was no link either of them knew of that bracketed the American Department of Education and foreign equivalents.

"I don't mean to be pessimistic but this whole thing is coming across a bit suspicious. I'm glad that you want to get into astronomy. Still, I think your mother and I would feel better if we could look up the information ourselves," Charles stated in a direct tone.

Their skepticism was warranted. Truthfully, the scholastic drafting was shrouded in mystery to even Julien. There were a few scenarios that could explain it. Frederick Douglass Junior High had eight principals in the last three years. One of them, bragging about the quality of their students, could have told someone who told someone in England his name and how he memorized the periodic table in a day. Maybe, during one of the national science fair conventions he took first place in, scouts from Edenshire Academy had been invited to watch. Or it really could have been fate. Whatever it was, the worries of his parents had to be curbed to make it come to fruition.

"That's not a problem. I have what they sent here with me. Maybe you can check it out after you're done with dinner," Julien suggested, handing over the letter.

Charles sighed, took the paperwork, and looked at Sandra. He scanned the wording and slid it to her. Julien could have guessed that there was something on his father's mind, but he was never one to talk about his feelings. He was a traditionalist. Bottling up emotions and pretending to be made of stone was what he did. He never cried, not even when Sandra miscarried her second pregnancy. It was strange for Julien to see him on the verge of tears.

"I am overjoyed to be your father. You're growing up fast and sometimes, I wish you'd stop. I think, if it's alright with your mother, that being away for a summer would build your independence," he admitted, tapping his fork at the center of an empty plate.

Sandra rubbed Charles's knee to stop him from gouging the dinnerware. His fidgeting was a nervous twitch. Sentimental moments were uncomfortable for him. When he was a third semester senior at Morgan State University, he proposed to her with a poem and all ten of his fingers trembled. His friends and co-workers mythicized him as a tough guy, but she knew his weak spots. Herself and Julien were his world. If a disaster ever befell them, he would break into pieces that were too small to reassemble. A loyal member of a team, she backed him.

"We can't hold you forever. Whether we like it or not, you'll be done with high school soon and off to college. Howard and North Carolina A&T already interviewed us about your 1520 on the SAT," she explained. "If this is what you want to do, I will support it, Juju."

Julien scooted toward his parents and wrapped them in his arms. They weren't going to try to deter him. Excitedly chatting about a realistic alternative to his lifelong ambition to be the protege of Bill Nye, he seemed captivated by the prospect of impending endeavors. His conscience told him that he was at fault for deceiving them, but the purpose transcended morality. Besides, the way he saw things, they would not know he went for an ulterior motive. He'd find

Jean-Renee's grave, search for clues to the formulas, and be on the next train to Edenshire Academy. Convincing them to let him go was the hard part and he triumphed without hassle.

A three-person hug unified the Preux trio. There was encouragement for the emotional duo to view the online brochure, as they were left with the letter. When their son turned to leave, Charles wiped his dampened eyes. The child who emulated him was becoming a man. His wife laid her head on his meaty shoulder, that short brier of kinky hair tickling his collar bone. She swiped teardrops away and stroked his thickset chest through the black Omega Psi Phi hooded jersey cushioning it. Her touch was magical, soothing him more effectively than any prescribed sedative.

"I see a lot of you in him, Charles. He has your smarts and resourcefulness. He's going to grow up to change the world, just you wait and see," Julien heard his mother say as he disappeared up the staircase.

The silence that met him at the top floor was momentarily interrupted by the ticking noise of an email notification. Thinking that it could have been from Emmanuel, he darted to his bedroom. Hunching, he looked at his Hushmail inbox and saw that it was from Edenshire Academy. He reckoned that it was an automated message. The time zone difference between the United States and England meant that it was unlikely anyone was available to file an application.

"Dear Mister Julien Michel Preux, it is an esteemed pleasure to admit you into our annual summer enrich-

ment program. One of our representatives will be corresponding with you shortly to confirm an appropriate date and time for an in-person screening. An introductory packet is now being prepared for you. Inside of it, you will find directions to our school, a preview of the vast choices in food that we offer, and a gallery of our recreational pastimes, which include but are not limited to: Brazilian Jiu-Jitsu, calligraphy, choir, football, fencing, gymnastics, photojournalism, weight training, and welding. There will also be a parental consent form to be signed and returned to us either before or after your screening. Please do not hesitate to reach out to us with any questions that you may have. We look forward to welcoming you to our ranks."*

Julien blinked, so astonished with the speedy reply that the lack of a signature in the closing went unnoticed. The email, in the midst of being forwarded to his parents, was clicked out of. They had enough hearing about him leaving for one evening. Taking them any further through the ringer would be overkill. He still had to share the news with his cousin. Patting his pockets for his Samsung Galaxy, he almost fainted when it was not located. 4Chan memes, illegally downloaded music, and pirated apps were stored on that device.

Panic had Julien peering in search of his book bag. Slumped by the chimney, he snatched the zipper back and thumbed through lab reports, sighting the expensive gadget at the bottom. Relief set in. He recalled it was slipped in there at lunch to avoid damage during a cafeteria dessert fight. The battery was at zero but it was not lost. The cord to the charger connected to the socket was seized and stuck in before it was sat on the dresser. Five minutes of power and it would be back up and running. He opted to send Emmanuel an email ahead of getting ready to shower.

Unceremonious disrobing left Julien's clothes tossed in a messy pile. An ear was kept out for nearing movement. Being caught in the nude by his parents was not on his bucket list. Hearing a discussion about Theresa May and Brexit, he knew they were distracted. Their voices mustered optimism about England's viability for his internal growth. Tiptoeing naked as they talked about the modules, he entered the bathroom.

The tiled floor was cold. Clorox bleach mopped it thoroughly, he figured, judging by the slight irritation in his nose. Started by a turn of the shower latch, hot rain fell. The only cloth from the rack was fair game. A full bottle of Old Spice body wash sat on the sink counter. He stepped in and lathered himself in blue soap for an extensive cleaning. A walk home in ninety-degree weather was a recipe for sweaty armpits if there ever was one.

Cleansed of the smell of fried onions, he covered himself with a cotton towel, and went back to his bedroom, leaving behind a drippy trail.

The square knot that held the towel up was released once the door closed. Wiping the water droplets off his broadening body of mocha flesh, Julien rolled on a stick of Herban Cowboy deodorant to keep the odors of testosterone at bay. Spiderman briefs from a laundry hamper donned, a yawn of exhaustion signaled bedtime. A new hazy projection of the man with a ruined reputation spawned in his dreams.

On bent and abraded knees, he rocked inside a chalk circle that was decorated with elaborate shapes. Head bowed, his face remained unseen but his knuckles were soaked in blood. Laying at his knees was a panther chameleon. Its hind legs, broken and crooked, were massaged by the man. Miraculously, the limbs straightened and the reptile crawled away from him. It then laid an exceptionally large egg, which was lifted by the man and held over his head.

Awaking to a backhand against his forehead, Julien's eyes opened and squinted. Rays of sunshine blazed, blinding him. He did not think he slept the whole night, but his morning breath said otherwise. Thirsty, he was dehydrated and being checked by Sandra, who took on the role of resident doctor.

"Mom, why are you waking me up so early? Today's Saturday and I don't have any tutoring sessions for French. The school year's over."

"It's five minutes to ten, sweetie pie. I would have let you keep sleeping, but you were hollering about exchange laws. You must've been dreaming you were an economics professor. I came in to make sure you didn't have a fever."

The details of Julien's dream replayed in slow motion. Banks, debit cards, credit repairs, and gross income were absent. Night terrors were not hereditary in the Preux family. The diagnosis of a sleep disorder would put a halt on the journey that had not even began.

"Listening to podcasts that quote Bill Maher and Stephen Colbert must have side effects. Fortunately, I wasn't quoting Donald Trump, huh," Julien awkwardly laughed, striving to make light of the situation.

Sandra rose from the edge of the bed. She was cloaked in the robe she left the hospital in after giving birth. The plaid covering, gifted to her by a Haitian nurse, was a memento that she would never part with. It was one of many reminders that she had a special boy.

"You have a visitor. She's been here for an hour, waiting for you to wake. I think you'd like to hear what she has to say," she informed, winking over her shoulder.

Julien smeared the sweat off his face once he was alone. Grabbing a Washington Redskins t-shirt and matching sweatpants from the same hamper his underwear came out of, he plucked crud from his eye crevices and sleepily waddled downstairs.

In the living room, a woman sat on the leather couch beside Charles. She had high cheek bones and voluminous chestnut hair that was tied into a ponytail. An orange sheath dress accentuated her frame, but showed no cleavage and hid just enough of her tanned thighs to not be racy. The debut of the individual she came to see caused her to shift those smoky gray eyes toward him.

"My name is Tatyana Rusev. I sent you the initial email. Typically, I don't conduct in-person interviews but I saw your credentials, and I knew that I had to meet you!"

It was Saturday morning but she was wide awake. Most would have been slobbering on their pillows or scarfing down breakfast. Here she was, well-rested, even though her flight to the United States had to have been hours long and cost a fortune on such short notice. Still groggy, Julien extended his hand to her.

She accepted it, a straw bracelet with a wolf's head as its single charm shuffling on her wrist.

"Nice to meet you. Sorry for the messiness. Had I known you were coming, I would have at least gargled," he admitted, getting everyone to laugh.

Tatyana adjusted the Juicy Couture bag on her left shoulder, making it easier to reach inside as she spoke.

"Your father was curious about how Edenshire Academy found you. To make a long story short, the article that you wrote about cattle cloning was published in many science journals. For someone who does not hold a degree, you are incredibly eloquent. We were quite impressed. Since then, we've seen you collect many awards and a simple Google search led us right to you. You are the first American we've pinged in two years."

A homework assignment from 2015 had made a junior high schooler a hot commodity. Charles always said adults in education thrived on association with youths that were perceived to be geniuses. He claimed it was an avenue for them to accomplish what they couldn't in their own adolescence. Yet, there was sincerity in the statements that spilled off her Slavic tongue.

"I realize that this meeting was impromptu and I did not mean to be an intrusion. I stopped by to get an authentic representation of you and your family. That is part of the on-boarding we don't include in the emails. You're a wonderful example of what we value most at Edenshire Academy: love. I'd like to present you with these," Tatyana declared.

Out of her purse came a laminated folder. A holographic embroidery of the school's coat of arms was in the center.

"I must be going now. It is my understanding that traffic here can be very, very intimidating. Your airline ticket and compulsory documentation are inside. The flight is in exactly one week. You are doing a greater service than you know."

With three firm handshakes and a flash of her pearly white teeth, she was gone. The Preuxs did not move nor speak. The protective veil around Julien was set to be lifted. The deal was done.

CHAPTER II

*J*une 10, 2017 was the date. Broad strokes of violet painted the skyline. Beneath the morning's guise were twin rows of vehicles that cluttered the I-295 highway. Honking horns startled drivers who fell asleep at the wheel. Profane insults were exchanged when inattentive texters narrowly avoided close calls, swerving. The ensuing chaos threatened the scheduled flights of poorly-planned travelers.

Had Sandra not known the misfortune that was reorganizing vacations because of lateness, Julien would have been counted among the masses that were detained in a stagnant TSA line. A glitch in programming had stopped the conveyor belt's functioning. As technical support staff tinkered with the mechanical chambers, unscrewing nuts and bolts, complaints surged. Their grouchy attitudes were pointless. Laws reigned indisputable, even in the worlds of the most self-absorbed.

"If anything comes up, text me. I need to know you landed safely, too, so tell me when you're in Newcastle," she said, unloading Julien's suitcase from the trunk of her Mercedes-Benz.

A tight hug was all Sandra had to tie her over until

he came back in August, a return she desperately anticipated once he parted the entry door to the Grand Cosmopolitan Airport.

Business obligations prevented Charles from coming. The revered doctor verbally committed to hosting a urological conference in San Francisco last February, per the request of a former intern. A send-off benefaction in the form of five hundred dollars was meant to make amends for missing his son's big day.

A cinnamon bun cured sorrows that were dormant within Julien. He strove to not dirty the fuchsia Ralph Lauren V-neck he saved for the occasion, but nice clothing and a rumbling stomach were never an ideal mix. The warm, gooey roll was irresistible Its sweet aroma was hypnotic, entrancing with buttery swirls. A plastic fork and knife sliced it in half, the two sides dripping with icing.

"Now boarding passengers for flight 115 with service to Newcastle. Those in group one, first-class, and active duty U.S. military with identification, please have your tickets out," a British Airways employee announced, resting her flabby forearms on the desk in front of her.

In a single file line, men and women assembled. Some were dressed in suits and ties, while others looked more casual. One man, pasty with black spiked hair, sported tawdry neck tattoos and double septum piercings. The employee mistook him for the lead singer of Papa Roach, requesting an autograph and a selfie. He was not amused.

Julien devoured the remains of the cavity-inducing treat, tossing its box and utensils in the wastebasket carried by a passing custodian. Butterscotch-colored Timberlands moving, he dabbed his face with a napkin and joined the crowd. The luggage he dragged behind him rolled, its wheels blinking.

"Have a nice day and enjoy your flight, sir," said the employee assigned to scan barcodes.

The corridor that led into the airplane did so by curving right, where two stewardesses monotonously welcomed passengers. Their makeup-caked faces feigned thrilled expressions.

First-class was luxurious. There was enough room to belch, and not have the person next to you be able to guess what you ate. Haggling for carry-on space in the overhead bins was not a normality. The suites came equipped with a personal power supply for electronics, which meant web browsing and listening to music was not on a limited tap.

Seat 1A was reserved for Julien. Solo, its black cushion begged to be rested upon. The pull-out bed variation it included was an added perk. Temptation to nap was seductive, but he was brimming with energy from superficial carbohydrates. Hoisting his property, he enclosed it in the compartment above him. Passengers in cabins further back glared with envy, lugging their belongings through the rows. Sinking into comfort, he plugged in the headphones of his vintage iPod, shutting out the instructions of a stewardess in the case of an emergency. He heard how to board evacuation rafts a million times; it was pantomimed every occasion he flew.

Julien sat patiently during the pre-flight taxiing phase. One after another, pilots steered airplanes like gigantic aluminum clusters. Bored, he read the seat pamphlets that documented legal airline conditions and rules put in place to reduce the frequency of fatalities.

Following yellow lines drawn on the pavement, the momentum stopped at the starting line of the runway. Piston engines ran at high-power, screaming a windy battle cry. Acceleration was rapid, enabling a swift ascension. The climb to a 30,000-foot altitude had commenced. That was the best part to Julien. He adored watching the ride over towering skyscrapers. As it was seven in the morning on a clear Saturday, he could see the decreasing size differences unfiltered. A cruise on top of the clouds, though, would eventually rob him of that privilege. Blankness was going to be the solitary outer view for nine and a half hours.

Time ticked away. They rode unruffled. The plane's steadily straightforward flow facilitated routine aisle checks from the stewardesses, who maneuvered through crannies, serving snacks and alcohol on a food cart. They later passed out immigration cards to be signed by passengers who were not citizens of the United Kingdom. The navy-blue tint of raised shades was engulfed by blackness that spread expeditiously, gnawing at the evening glow like a ravenous animal. Nightfall approached.

Two cups of Starbucks iced coffee had Julien wired. Thumbs twiddling, the classic rock playlist that blared in his ears grew stale. His body craved to be exercised. Since cartwheeling was presumably discouraged, meandering to the bathroom stall would have to do. The chance of observing a couple join the mile-high club was improbable, but influential in his decision-making. Just as he reached for the belt buckle, the winds grew fierce. Turbulence rocked the plane leftward. One stewardess, now animated by her real temperament, pacified the fearful.

"Make sure y'alls belts is fastened. Not too far off from landing now so bear with us," she pleaded, her vocal pitch cracking and southern.

The tenseness of the moment intensified with a wicked boom. Thunder wailed and halted all conversations. One strike of lightning hit and the engine was instantly on fire. A billowing haze began to fill the cabins. Julien, in unison with his peers, clawed at the ceiling for the masks those emergency videos highlighted.

Pervading vapors dissolved, but did not stop various passengers aboard flight 115 from ripping their life preservers out of the packaging and huffing as they filled the tubes with air. Families whimpered, arms encasing them in sobbing huddles. A Muslim man in the seat opposite of Julien clutched a leather-bound Quran, praying aloud. The silk kufi atop his head fell off, tumbling afield.

"If I would've just listened to my dad, I wouldn't be here. I'm gonna die and they won't find my body," Julien whispered regretfully, biting his nails.

Staggering in an unanticipated storm, the plane sharply dipped to 18,000-feet. An unmistakably English intonation interrupted Julien's soliloquy. It came from the Muslim man. With the book that was sacred to him pressed to his brown dashiki, he referenced a key fact about aeronautics.

"Allah has not left us. I saw a documentary on the telly about planes; they can fly with one engine."

Julien then realized that death was a unifying concept. It did not distinguish between color, creed, gender, financial status, or political affiliation. Social constructs were non-factors when a person's hourglass emptied. They were the same: human. Questions of survival ran rampant until the order came from the pilot to assume the emergency landing position. Coughing, Julien bent over and grabbed his ankles. He heard the stewardesses yell a command.

"Brace for impact!"

The clunky wheels of the undercarriage ejected and raked the tarmac at Newcastle Imperial Airport. Firetrucks sped onto the premises, sirens distorting the tranquil night. Outside of the portholes, passengers could see water from the nozzle of high-powered hoses breaking apart flames on the burning areas. Ladders lifted the rescuers that brandished extinguishers, guiding their sprays. Black smoke danced, wiggling into the sky. Julien, hearing gleeful ovations, sat up in relief. It did not matter that his neck ached; he was happy to be alive.

Earphones still plugged in, he looked down to see fragments of his iPod. It was shattered, having slid below his boots during the rough descent. The tracks he transferred and deleted from his laptop were gone. Under normal circumstances, it would have been a pity to see an item that revolutionized technology crushed, but tonight was surreal. Life was more precious than any contraption sold in stores.

"Folks, the scary weather gave us some problems with the engine but we're going to be just dandy," the pilot declared. "We've arrived at our destination. The local time is 11:15pm. Be kind and courteous to those around you on the way out. Thanks for booking with British Airways, and we hope to see you again real soon."

Julien stood on wobbly legs after he was freed from the seatbelt. One stewardess scrambled from the front of the aircraft to the back, surveying the injuries for reports. All were minor. The Jacoby Shaddix lookalike suffered a busted nose but did not make a fuss. The worst thing she saw was vomit in seat 24C. It was a chunky puddle of green vomit that no passenger admitted to expelling.

"I appreciate you talking to me back there," Julien told the Muslim man, reclaiming his luggage.

When the stewardess standing by the cockpit was notified that it was safe for passengers to begin exiting, Julien was the first to leave. Traumatic events were the building blocks of religious persuasions. The Preux men were tolerant of all faiths, but had historically been atheists. Science was their dogma. Charles told Julien the views of atheism were not to be chatted about with strangers, because fewer feelings got hurt if immortalized beings were not debunked by meticulous data.

Honoring Sandra's request superseded partaking in conversations Julien could not care less about. Polite waves were given to the stewardess tag team in his transition. He caught glimpses of their faces when he glanced up from typing the text message. They could have auditioned for sad clowns with their streaked makeup and wild hair. Those disheveled appearances told an unforgettable incident, one that would not be added to the short sentence on the telephone's screen.

Employees that worked for mainly Europe-servicing

airlines were sprinkled in booths. Most were busy, providing timetables for baggage claim and terminal numbers. Electronic signs directed recent arrivals where to proceed. The first stop was border control. Divided into two sections, one queue was for European Union Nationals and the second for all others.

Flight 115's passengers trickled in behind Julien, who poked around the undergarments that were packed in with his belongings. His passport, originally positioned on top of everything, was misplaced. He found it sticking out of a heap of Nike socks. The plane's extreme rocking had to have been the culprit.

"Sir, step forward with your passport or identity card in your hand," a raspy-voiced officer said, coughing in his booth.

His consistent sniffling meant he was battling a cold. Dealing with incompetent people while being sick tended to bring out the worst in dispositions. Julien, not wanting to aggravate him, hurried to present the small blue book.

Gloved fingers flipping through the pages, the officer was impressed with how many countries Julien had visited.

"Aye, you've been around the world and back," he remarked. "What brings you to Newcastle?"

Julien assumed that his immigration card, which lay on top of his passport, would have been satisfactory. Unwilling to start an altercation, he casually leaned onto the luggage's handle and cleared his throat.

"I'm just here for a summer enrichment program with Edenshire Academy. I'll be studying astronomy."

"You must be quite the boy genius then," the officer concurred, stamping the passport. "Tried to enroll me daughter thrice and was denied every time."

His crystal blue eyes narrowed and were fixated on Julien's luggage. He had seemingly contemplated supplemental evaluation but, having stamped his passport, reconsidered.

"Be cognizant of the signs. They'll guide you to public transportation. Buses are cheaper than trains," he informed, returning the passport.

Julien tucked it between his stomach and jeans, drifting onward. Turning the corner, he heard the officer sneeze. The splattering sound of mucus gave him an incentive to walk faster: germs were heatseeking missiles.

He utilized an escalator to access the ground-level. Advertisements for employment firms, fast food, golf tournaments, and wireless internet hung along the walls in abundance. A flashing board stretched over a row of glass panels. The words "Shuttle Service" flickered in orange before a rundown of the scheduled departures. Each had dropped blinds with the exception of the fifth. Behind it sat a young man, fidgeting with the buttons of an over-sized red vest. The incessant movement stopped when he became aware that he was being watched.

"How can I help?" he asked, speaking into a microphone.

"I'm trying to get to Cumberchester Heights. Are there any buses that will take me there, or at least somewhere near it?"

Julien's inquisition intrigued the ticket salesman. His pronunciation gave him away as an American.

"Why yi wanna gan there?" he prodded, unlocking the drawer beside him. "Most young travelers go to see the Tyne Bridge or the city center. Cumberchester Heights is a dying seaside village. Everyone who lives there is old or mentally handicapped. Resorts that set up shop there always end up bankrupt. It's where people go to die."

Julien knew his story had to be finessed. Graveyard excursions were rarely on the average traveler's to-do list. Spooked locals had a knack for getting the police to snoop around outsiders.

"My great-grandpa is buried there. I didn't get to meet him before he died, but I'd like to pay my respects," he stated, fishing in his pocket for his wallet.

The ticket salesman bowed his head in sympathy. Sticking his arm through the oval-shaped hole at the bottom of the glass, he opened his hand to reveal a stub.

"Losing a relative can be depressing, but I'm sure he was a proper canny bloke," he said. "Take it, the last bus will be coming soon."

His random act of kindness took Julien aback. He was prepared to pay the full price of a ticket and any additional taxes for short notice. The fuss of buses driving out of the station soon had him spying over his shoulder. He bid the ticket salesman farewell and went outside, beholding clouds that smothered the moon.

Nighttime in Newcastle upon Tyne had an eccentric exoticism. Drunken slurs of filthy slang echoed in the distance, unmarred by shrieking tires. British flags flapped on top of hostels and restaurants, intermixed with Geordie pride placards. Barricades around the bus bays were tagged with graffiti that promoted anarchy. He thought everything deserved to be photographed.

Burst mode on Julien's telephone captured all the grit and glory. Arm swaying left to right and topsy-turvy, the memory card hit capacity. Crouching, he Snapchatted the curb where a cutworm slithered. His filming stopped when thong sandals kicked at him.

Sat on a wooden bench was a strawberry blonde girl, fiddling with a pink spiked necklace. Her emerald gaze was unrelenting. She laughed when Julien swore he was not a voyeur.

"Do ya fancy yaself a photographer?" she teased, slipping a gumball into her mouth.

Had Julien been fair-skinned, his cheeks would have flushed red. He was an obvious tourist. The only things omitted were a fanny pack, binoculars, and a map. Nervously rubbing the nape of his neck, he put the cellular phone away.

"I'm just havin' a go at ya," she admitted. "Whereabouts are ya from, cameraman?"

"Washington D.C. It's where the president lives!"

The chance for Julien to redeem himself made excitement emanate from each syllable. One utterance of his hometown's prestigious monuments would impress her, he thought. A blown bubble rained on that parade. Before he further bored her, she steered the conversation in a new direction.

"I ain't seen many spiffy Americans like ya here since I moved from London. Feds got tired of me robbin' people in Southwark. Get bad habits when ya hav'ta pay for medicine yourself because your mum's a drug addict."

Julien disregarded her admission of crime as ineffective hype. The first comment, whether intentional or not, was taken as a compliment.

"Thanks for noticing. I'll be studying at Edenshire Academy for the summer, but I also need to go to a cemetery in Cumberchester Heights."

Jaw dropping, the green-eyed girl transferred the suitcase that sat next to her to the ground. Patting the space it once occupied, she invited her new friend to sit.

"I've just returned from the dullest holiday to my nan's in Cyprus," she said. "You've gotta tell me what ya got goin' on!"

As she rattled off theories of what he could be up to, Julien smiled. He had successfully impersonated an undercover Satanic missionary. Each of the corny independent horror movies he watched came in handy. Now, he just had to play it cool; giving up the truth would dilute his mystique.

"I don't even know who you are. Why would I tell you my business?" Julien quizzed, suggesting a proper introduction.

"Cuz we're gonna be schoolmates at Edenshire and if you don't, I'll tell everyone I saw ya eatin' bugs," she countered. "I'm Blair, by the way. Charmed to meet ya."

Meeting new acquaintances prior to a teacher's icebreakers was alien to Julien. Blair's sassy yet comical threats gave her an ambiance snooty American girls lacked. She was not quite a tomboy nor a diva. The brash beauty was in a class of her own, blurring the lines. Enticed, he told her his name and stuck his hand out for a shake, but abruptly rescinded it when static electricity coursed through his palm.

"Forgive me. That's happened a lot lately. Has to

do with electrons, I read," she smirked.

Julien knew that explaining how bodies built up an imbalance of electrical charges would be too nerdy. It was commonplace knowledge in his school that no guy ever received a hands-on lesson in the reproductive organs by invoking Albert Einstein.

Lights beamed as the bus pulled in. The two boarded, passing snoring passengers on their way to the back. They shared embarrassing stories to make the time go by. Ones that involved botched shavings and wardrobe mishaps in front of their cousins were funniest to them. Their conversation's tone became somber when they drove past a billboard for women's health.

The scent of peppermint sweetened Blair's breath. Her lips, thin and wet, demanded attention. Devoid of cracks, they were impeccable in rendering Julien stupid. Her revelation of being a 15-year-old ovarian cancer survivor traced the smitten boy's eardrums. He was under a spell of empathetic lust.

"Come on then, let's hear it. I'm waitin' to know what you're goin' to the cemetery for!"

The authoritative dazzle in that proclamation snapped Julien out of hypnosis. He had to come clean. He told Blair about the many charismatic personalities in his family, and she commented how they were the perfect example of kinship. Omitting the most significant bit was unconscionable, given how candid she was with him.

"Jean-Renee Preux was the name of my great-grandfather. Everybody wants to forget he existed. I'm not going to let that happen, not unless I find out he really was a crook."

The surroundings changed with each stop on the route, drained of glamour. Pubs became rare. Shops were no different. Barren fields were the only constants. The bus driver's vocal reminder that there were just two stops before the end of the line woke both teenagers from their catnap.

"Scoot," Blair ordered, tugging Julien out of his seat and into the chilly night.

An abundance of Gothic, moss-covered houses greeted them. Shoddy lampposts shined on the street, unveiling a tarnished bronze plaque. Like moths to a flame, they inched toward it.

"Blythe Gardens. That's the only cemetery in town," Blair said.

"Guess you know this place pretty well. Feel free to lead," Julien responded.

"It's just up ahead but I doubt anyone is there to help us. Time to put on our detective hats, cameraman!"

Abysmal were the odds of locating a specified grave without qualified assistance. It was of no consequence that Blythe Gardens was the only cemetery in Cumberchester Heights; Jean-Renee was one number in an unknown chronology.

Fading stars stole more moonlight, enlarging shadows for nightmare fuel. Blair's navigation turned those adversities moot. She walked with confidence, head high like a seasoned heroine. Her strength was infectious, spreading to Julien's heart. Side by side, they descended a dimly lit path. A wide lot, cuddled by razor wire fences, was the prize for their bravery.

The rusted gate creaked open, leaves fluttering under it. Ravens mobbed a decaying evergreen at the entrance, flying higher and higher to roost on branches. Their caws sang a baleful symphony, the lyrics grim with omens.

"This may not be a good idea, now that I think about it. We'll come back in the morning. You know, when the groundskeeper is around and our chances of being stewed decrease," Julien proposed, backpedaling to make an about-face.

Pinched by the lobe of his ear, he was escorted into the cemetery by Blair.

"Move your ass," she shouted, leaving their luggages unattended at the front.

The lack of upkeep was disheartening. Beer bottles were tangled in weeds. Stale feces laid in plain sight. Mildew deteriorated asymmetrical gravestones. Somewhere in that putrid hellhole was Jean-Renee.

Aimless wandering resulted in a split to cover more ground. Their shoes imprinted mud, nightcrawlers writhing as they were trotted on.

"Sucks they won't honor his memory," called out Blair.

Julien, wiping dirt off a marker, endured another disappointment. The deceased were harder to find than the living. A dead man capable of inciting a wild goose chase was one who personified clout.

"My dad says he got rich because he swindled people into thinking he could turn anything gold," Julien replied, uprooting from a crouch. "It probably sounds silly, but I have these dreams and I think they're telling me something."

Buzzing, Julien's barely charged telephone lit up

like a Christmas tree. Sandra bombarded him with cloned text messages. A generic script of "I'm fine, don't worry" lies was delivered before the device died. Out of his peripheral vision, he saw Blair's flailing arms.

"I think you might want to see this," she hollered.

Jogging, Julien reunited with her at the site of a smashed marble obelisk. Engraved across the shaft was the name of Jean-Renee Preux. Mouth wide open, Julien circled the object, investigating every detail. Dates were blotched but the number seven, merged with an infinity sign, was intact.

"That symbol, I've seen it before. It's in the note-pad that my great-grandfather had. I have it in my luggage, I'll show you," he swore.

Sudden snarls streaked freezing terror down their spines. Amber eyes unblinking, a purple wolf with matted fur strode from behind a crumbling mausoleum. Bearing jagged fangs, the canine salivated.

"Wolves ain't been in England for absolutely ages," Blair gulped. "What the bloody hell is one doin' here?"

"Let's consult Animal Planet if we make it outta here alive. Run!"

They bolted. Blair was a blur. Galloping strides prolonged her survival. Mindful of the increasing gap, Julien raced to catch up. Ahead by an inch, the pitter-patter of her feet was thunderous. A downward glance unearthed glints of electricity looping around her toes. Visible expulsion of charged particles beckoned marvel, but a starving predator endangered their lives.

Barks sent vibrations through their knees, the beast hot on their heels. Lactic acid weakening their joints, the pace at which they ran gradually declined.

Wheezing scuttles ceased at a pile of barbed tape where rats nested. Climbing was not an option. The wolf's muzzle throbbed with hunger when the pair turned to meet their apparently impending demise. A quick lunge launched spiky teeth at Julien's jugular. His flinching arms rose in horror to block. Eyes clenched, his hands lost all sensation. Layers of copper shielded his elbows. On impact, the wolf disintegrated. A reverberating howl signified its defeat. Blair stood speechless, her small breasts heaving.

"I have no idea how," she started. "But you killed the bugger."

"I get queasy from dissecting frogs. I don't ever wanna see my own limbs severed," admitted Julien, patting himself.

"I feel ya, but what the hell's goin' on, bruv? It's a mad 'ting," said Blair.

"We should leave right now. As much as I hate to say it, this cemetery must be cursed," Julien hypothesized, gawking at her luminous sandals.

Their escape was thwarted by tremors. The tiny purple segments that were once the wolf steamed. Mist thickened, twisting like a hurricane whilst a visage manifested. Puckered lips blew a gust that cocooned the duo, whisking them under a nocturnal rainbow.

CHAPTER III

Oceanic hymns thrummed, waves sensually caressing a nearby shore. Diving otters remixed the tune with energetic splashes. The midnight melody rocked Julien and Blair asleep in that vaporous farce of a cradle. They were snuggled like twin babies on a cherry hardwood floor.

A chill awakened them.

"Where have we been taken?" asked Blair.

The prompt shifting irked Julien, who relished in her warmth. Dazed, he massaged his temples and looked around in confusion. Rhinestone chandeliers hung above them. Blue velvet rugs covered a pristine staircase. Weathered bookcases stretched along freshly painted beige walls. Adjacent to them was a triangular door that was decorated with a mistletoe.

"Looks like some fancy hotel's lobby, but I doubt this is the Four Seasons or the Beaumont," he said.

The unmistakable cocking of gun hammers paralyzed them. Heavy tramping brought an elderly gentleman dressed as a priest down the stairs. He twirled dual nine-millimeter pistols. His salt and pepper beard and sunglasses likely made him look more like a desperado than a servant of God.

Whistling, he juggled the firearms. First, they went

in a circular cycle, caught and tossed by their barrels. The theatrics quickly became more fantastical, incorporating spins and a bowing finale. Both clips fell out and his head rose.

"Not exactly, lad. You're at Edenshire Academy."

The likelihood of being shot terrorized Julien and Blair. One slip of a crusty finger could have sent hollow-point bullets right through their crowns. When they loudly sprawled onto their palms and knees, the gunman arched a brow. Head shaken, he threw down his weapons.

"An ol' Brummie like myself forgets his manners often. Father Nigel Mortimer Bradshaw, at your service!"

"Tellin' us you're from Birmingham don't mean nothin'," said Blair, loading a clip into one of the guns and aiming at the crucifix pinned to his white collar. "I been to the West Midlands and even them church-goers hit up brothels."

Julien sat silently, braced for a bang. He never saw a stick-up in person. Movies portrayed it dramatically, slow and laced with graphic language. That was wrong. It all happened in a jumble. A priest went from an ordained official to potential target practice in a split second.

Blair spat her gum at him. "Don't be stupid. Let us go and I won't shoot ya, old man."

Father Nigel placed his hands on the floor, hangnail-infested fingers spread wide open. He was at her mercy.

"Dear Lord, neither of you are being forced to stay against your free will. You may leave at any time you wish, but you won't get the answers that you seek."

Honesty purified the priest's expression. There was no beaming grin or scathing grimace, only the wrinkles of a face that saw decades of stress. Julien, bewildered by the series of eerie happenings, needed to know what he knew. He patted Blair's thigh and she lowered the pistol but did not release it.

"If I were you, sir, I'd start talking fast."

Father Nigel's head bobbed graciously. Straightening from a hunch, he paced back and forth. Blair watched him like a hawk.

"There is a host of knowledge that you must internalize briskly. We haven't much time to begin your courses," he declared, stroking his chin.

"I've had enough of your lies," growled Blair, propping Father Nigel's nose up with the gun barrel. "You sent that letter to my flat cuz you were lookin' for somebody to kidnap. This ain't no school."

Suddenly, electricity revolved around her wrists. The hotheaded girl's jaw dropped.

Father Nigel felt the static and remarked, "Your body is having another involuntary reaction, similar to what happened in the cemetery. I can educate you on how to control your grace."

Risk of splattered brains did not affect the unorthodox priest's tone. There was a fiery conviction in his enunciation, erupting from the very fibers of his soul. Julien, staggering to his feet, wedged himself into the mix.

"Grace?"

"Elements have graced you," Father Nigel explained. "That is the source of her electricity and your metal."

Red and brown blends of armor had fortified Julien's arms, his recollection of being hunted vivid. He knew that impenetrable skin was not a byproduct of hormones; maturing boys became sexually active, not metallic. A dissertation of how the ludicrous concept was a slap in the face to science was on the horizon. Mentally, he formulated religion-attacking, blasphemous insults but none came. He chose not to replicate his father's skepticism, feeling that the power of belief in itself was mystical.

"Elaborate."

Taking a deep breath, Father Nigel removed those dark shades. His eyes were a milky white. He was blind.

"Though you may not believe me, this is indeed a school. It is my sworn mission as an envoy to teach you all that I can about the peril that the Earth's resources are in. You are the pupils that will preserve the planet. Please, follow me."

Reluctantly, they trusted him. Julien noticed that the current around Blair's wrists vanished. Still, she kept the pistol in a firm grasp.

Close as shadows, the teenagers toured the estate. Impaired vision did not hinder Father Nigel's sense of direction. Turned corners revealed portraits of Parliament leaders, all of whom he expertly described by the materials used. Blindness apparently gave him a deeper connection to the five senses. He walked without falter, entering a small classroom that was lit by wax candles.

On the surface of a blackboard was a wall of neat, cursive writing in pink chalk. Antique desks, crafted from woodwork, were ordered in two rows of four. When the fleeting racket of their movement stopped,

Father Nigel asked Julien and Blair to sit. The rugged chairs were painful to their bottoms. Neither could imagine how any child could learn whilst sitting on those damn things, but assumed that was irrelevant to what they were about to be told.

"In the Alpha Days, darkness covered the world," the priest began. "The elements, which are living forces, have always existed. Their role was to expand and blindly shape what would become Earth. Their continuous growth bloated the darkness, causing it to explode. The explosion birthed the newest element: light, which allowed them to watch the world's formation. As humans came into existence, they witnessed the good and bad in mankind."

Father Nigel's verbatim memorization of the blackboard was impressive to them. Disability had not completely crippled him. He could still imitate a public speaker, evidenced by the undivided attention of Blair. She was utterly awe-stricken by his diction. Julien wondered if that was how he would look hearing one of Jean-Renee's stories.

"Unnatural pollution jeopardized their sustenance. To preserve themselves, they expelled half of their essences into the air. The particles then bonded with humans they deemed worthy. Their remaining consciousness was stored within the bodies of spawned children, the Celortus, who needed to be protected in order for the elements to continue functioning. You have been chosen as their newest protectors," Father Nigel concluded.

In recounting that obscure creation legend, Father Nigel dropped a bombshell, explosively mining inquiries.

"But I've seen ads for this school. What of the prospectus and the website?" Blair asked.

"The Celortus have altered their appearances throughout the eons. They are highly articulate, interchangeable beings, many switching from male to female at will. Their cleverness allows for Edenshire Academy to run smoothly, examination scores and all."

Blair's concerns were not addressed in the surplus of writing beside them. Father Nigel's response was original, not a robotic paraphrase of mysticism. He conducted himself in the manner of an authentic professor.

Julien thought that Father Nigel's humility differentiated him from the clergymen that masqueraded like demigods, collecting outrageous tithes from the destitute and demanding unmitigated obedience. The fibs he employed to stay low-key, however, had to be challenged.

"I don't want to come off condescending, but why would you be the one to know this?"

Father Nigel smeared his thumbprint across that crucifix pin. Head thrown back, he placed one hand over his heart.

"Lad, I'm an exorcist, tried and true. From Australia to Africa, I have cast demonic entities out of the innocent with bullets blessed by holy water. The last one left me blind. The Celortus chose me as an envoy because of my will to fight!"

Father Nigel's sermon glowed with dedication. Fires of piety ignited him into action. Cuticles becoming stained with chalk residue, an underhanded press opened the blackboard, parting it like a valley.

Ultraviolet rays twinkled and the trio was sucked into the orifice.

Eight childlike hollowed bodies sat in a circle, holding hands and convulsing. Infrared gasses substituted their internal organs. Hexagonal crystals whizzed past them, slipping through every color in the spectrum.

"Can they see us?" questioned Blair, backing away.

Father Nigel smiled at the question. Sunglasses gripped, he squatted and said, "See, hear, and smell, my dear. They'd like to be more personal with you but they're rejuvenating. Elements need to do it. Can't exist otherwise."

"This is mad. How do I go from a bus stop to findin' out I'm some kinda freak," wondered Blair, crossing her willowy arms over her grey Northumbria University sweatshirt. "It's like I'm stuck in a weird dream. None of this can be real. I sat through too many hours of therapy to let myself believe this."

She went to leave but her Achilles tendon was nabbed by a lukewarm hand.

"Heroism can be detected in you both, it seeps from your pores," Father Nigel told Julien and then pointed at his counterpart.

The face of the Celorti that grabbed Blair filled in. It was a little girl with shaggy, auburn hair and a missing front tooth.

"Please don't leave. The bad people are coming," she cried.

The Celorti's bottom lip quivered and Blair's green eyes watered.

"I always was a sucka for kids in need," she admitted. "Half of the money I looted in London went into the cups of poor kids so they could eat. What do I gotta do to help?"

Julien nodded. "Yeah, let us know."

Exhaling once the teenagers looked to him for more details, Father Nigel roamed the limestone chamber.

"The Oath Keepers. They're a cult of sorcerers who want to harness elemental energies to create a universe where only their race exists. Their true leader has not been seen, but he himself is graced by the rogue element of darkness. Victoria Gallows is their figurehead."

"Victoria Gallows? Why does that name sound so familiar?" inquired Blair.

The name in question had elicited a frightful reaction. Hissing like Madagascar cockroaches, the Celortus frenzied.

"She was a child prodigy from Belfast, a budding mathematician and classical flute player. Newspapers around the United Kingdom blogged about her talents. She was offered a place here at Edenshire Academy, but the Oath Keepers' leader blotted out the sun the day she was due to arrive. His minions intercepted the orientation, killed her parents, and stole her. She was indoctrinated and became a mascot for their sick fraternity," proclaimed Father Nigel.

The priest's role as an envoy implied that he was capable of nurturing. Julien, critical of his failure, was disposed to let accusations fly.

"If you're so divine, why didn't you stop them?" he angrily interrogated.

"That happened a year ago. The school was under the guidance of Rabbi Tov and Sister Agnieszka.

I did not come until he and two of his pupils were killed. It was on the eve of my final exorcism," explained Father Nigel.

Julien's contempt for religion did not outweigh logic. The alibi provided could not be argued against. He saw it unreasonable to fault a mortal man for not being present in multiple locations concurrently. He was set to apologize but Blair held the spotlight.

Crouching, she wrapped her arms around the weeping Celorti and nuzzled her.

"I watched a 2-year-old die from a brain tumor the day I was released from the hospital," Blair said. "I couldn't do anything for her, even though I wanted to so badly. This feels like my second chance to save somebody."

Skin of differing hues formed faces to the Celortus. Hair texture from wavy to coarse gave them distinctive traits, each uniquely beautiful. Interlocked, the hollowed bodies whirled, surrounding the teenagers.

"We believe in you," they crooned in a unified pitch.

Julien and Blair did not speak, a newly found boldness rendering them mute. Expressions had not yet been invented to accurately catalog doubt and boiling-hot blood on top of a suspicion of insanity. They were scared but knew there was no abandoning their solemn duties; they were chosen. An exchange of confirming nods solidified their devotion.

With the Celortus' faces reverting to see-through, a rift broke the ring. Father Nigel stood in the opening, pointing at the exit that was a breakaway wall. Edges dewy with blue gunk, swinging doors were a chore for the priest to paste back together. Veins popping in his forehead, he dry-heaved but succeeded.

"I commend you for undertaking this risky endeavor. I am honored to be your envoy," he stated, winded but walking.

From the classroom they departed. The pistol left lonely was returned to its rightful owner, hooked by Father Nigel on the way out. A subtle yellow sparkled through the windows of the hallway. It was the crack of dawn.

The teenagers goggled at the exquisite architecture before them. Their earlier rushed evacuation blocked cylinder vases on top of granite posts from their line of vision. Obsidian pillars reached to the second floor's compact balcony, sleek and unblemished.

"Are we the only ones?" asked Julien.

"Don't be yampy, lad. You've already met one of your classmates at the cemetery," Father Nigel said.

"You must be takin' the piss. We were the only people in Blythe Gardens," interjected Blair.

"Noah," Father Nigel clapped. "Join us and bring the uniforms we've put aside."

A chill dropped the hallway's temperature. Blowing down the staircase was that infamous mist. Lethargic, it touched one step at a time, pausing with sizzling vapors. Pulsating, the cloudy mass perished in a poof. A boy sat on a box at the foot of the stairs, silky platinum hair complementing his alabaster flesh. Knife cuts from the corners of his mouth stretched to his sideburns, scarring him with an everlasting smile.

A navy-blue polo was fitted to his skinny torso. The shirt featured an emblem of shields with wolf heads on both sides knitted in maroon, right above a ribbon banner that housed a row of stars. His tan, corduroy-clad legs were crossed one over the other, showing off his oxblood penny loafers. He winked one of those amber eyes and Julien deciphered Father Nigel's message.

"He was the face in the tornado that blew us out of the cemetery."

"And the wolf that chased yi, mate? That was me, too," Noah gloated, booting the box to the priest.

Doubling, Father Nigel stopped the sliding square with a stiff-arm. "Fella's graced by ectoplasm. It can be pesky in the hands of chaps with a dark sense of humor. Thirteen is a dreadful age," he huffed, peeling off the cardboard top.

"Ecto-what?" Blair spat out.

"Ectoplasm," chuckled Noah. "It's a windy element that gives ghosts a physical form. Not bad for illusions, either, seeing as how yi two headed for the hills!"

"Spankin' must not have been important in your home, I take it. Your mum and dad ought to smack some couth into ya thick skull," shrilled Blair.

The pale boy's face scrunched up and his head leaned onto the railing. No smart aleck rebuttal came.

Father Nigel, hearing the dispute, stopped foraging through the box and handed it to Julien.

"His parents, the Satterlys, were mediums that catered to a very niche clientele in Newcastle: family members of deceased psychopaths," the priest revealed. "The negative auras they conjured were gateways for revenants to enter this realm. One evening, they were used as vessels. I freed them of demonic control, but they went into cardiac arrest. The ambulances were too late."

Blair's cheeks went beet red. She was wholly embarrassed by her ignorant vitriol. Regretful, her eyes fell to the sheeny floor's intricate maze pattern. She told Noah that she was sorry, but he raised his hand in a shooing motion. Empty words, he branded them.

Julien's fascination with the crate gashed the growing balloon of tension. Copies of the uniform Noah sported were packed inside without a crease, accompanied by dress variations for girls. He vetted each and gave them a thumbs up.

"Never thought that I'd be fond of wearing the same threads as someone else but I have to admit, these are dope," he raved, sliding the box to Blair.

She stooped and had a look for herself. "You're right. I dig these."

Their favorable reviews pleased Father Nigel, who immediately claimed that a shared ensemble was key to any respectable faction, as it promoted camaraderie. He snapped and became the center of attention.

"The moment that you put those uniforms on, your lives will change forever. You'll become both, student and soldier. Your survival, much like my own, is not promised. Deadly tribulations await those who take up the task of preserving the elements. The world hinges on your earnest involvement in this eternal conflict. If, for even a millisecond, you think yourself fickle, I ask that you leave."

Tingling from nail to knuckle, Julien took a gander at his hands. They glittered with copper. Plausibility had been cast to the wayside. A pilgrimage to acquit his great-grandfather of wrongdoing had led him to self-discovery.

"This is where I belong," he confirmed.

Blair held a snakeskin belt, gazing at it as if willing herself to burn a hole straight through. Sparkles of electricity sprang from her palms, knocking the aluminum buckle clean off.

"I've wondered why I ain't dead like the other drillers. I know why now; I have a purpose."

Donning those dark shades, Father Nigel saluted them. Although he was blind, the priest said he visualized them as robust gladiators. It was a stark contrast to what they were, but he promised the right educator could morph even the unlikeliest of wards.

"Lectures will commence shortly. Noah will show you to your rooms. On your beds will be a textbook. Do familiarize yourselves with it and bring questions. I trust that you will be in uniform when next we meet," he said, waving goodbye.

The pale boy mutated into a cloud and breezed upward. Julien and Blair pursued him, their paths selected.

CHAPTER IV

Hatchlings chirped outside of Julien's window, a resounding plea for morning nourishment. Their mother, a Starling shone with the sun's florescence, littered their bulky nest with hairy spiders. Helplessly, the furred arachnids were guzzled. To see that raw, uninhibited mechanism in motion was the most succulent treat a connoisseur of experimentation could savor.

Mahogany vinyl lined the walls of a room that matched the square footage of a shabby studio apartment. A wooden dresser was posed beneath the windowsill, its drawers ripe with the fragrance of pine. A rectangular teak nightstand neighbored it, tattooed with pencil carvings of initials and country anagrams.

Charles would have been livid if he saw that Julien's eyelids were not pressed to the squeaky-clean glass.

"Forget the furniture; you are missing out on the beauty of the ecosystem, son," he'd say, devaluing all else.

The unremitting prattle of days elapsed was muted by the resplendent verses of an arcane scripture. Julien sat on the stiff linen of a folding cot, reclined with a book that was no bigger than a pocket Bible. Woven from sheepskin, it was leathery and featherweight. The cover, blank with the exception of minor craters, was iced brisk. Ruby gemstones adorned its spine.

Julien thought it strange how the major religions of the world never bewitched him with their epics of giants and dragons, yet this clandestine mythos beguiled him. Written in cephalopod ink was an origin gospel that lit his imagination ablaze. Paragraphs of aligned verses, indented and italicized, chronicled the Celortus' plight.

"Darkness, the archetype of all elementality, bears bastards from the oozing lesions of emerging luminescence. Vain and putrid, they glorify their creator with sacrifices of mucus and urine, pledging to revive the Alpha Days, an era of totalitarianism. They are the Mavkardia, forevermore a menace to terrestrial balance. Hallowed are the Elehominum who vow to vanquish them and their offshoots," he whispered, goosebumps layering his forearms.

Miniature portraits of multicultural youths, unsmiling and clothed in the uniform that Julien now wore, were systematized in a columned gallery at the bottom of every page. With the flip of each sheet, there were debuting faces but their biographies were absent. Appraising unmarked chapters, he lost himself in an avalanche of words but loud knocks stirred him. Rubber soles awkwardly settling on the floor, he nearly nosedived onto the handle of his luggage, which was recovered from Blythe Gardens by Noah. Father Nigel thought it a fitting penalty for his ghoulish prank.

Persistent knocking amplified the closer that Julien got to the door. Hammering bonks had him timidly reaching for the knob. It rotated smoothly and on the other side was a woman in full Carmelite nun garb, her hair veiled by a cream headdress. There was familiarity in her high cheek bones and pointy nose. It was Tatyana.

"I have a few..."

Julien was shushed with a finger pressed to his lips. Directed to follow, he walked into the hallway, where Blair leaned over a rail. Modeling a navy-blue dress on top of a white polo, she read from the same book he had clutched. A gentle tap on the shoulder was given to her and the two were soon tailing the nun, who hastily approached a busted grandmother clock. Dainty palms wrenching it to the far right, light glinted from the space left behind. She dipped in, her Velcro flats one-two tapping on steel.

"Dunking into a hole that leads to who knows where? Probably isn't smart."

Julien's pretentious assessment annoyed Blair. She turned to him, a glare reflecting off the Edenshire Academy emblem on the straps of her dress.

"We signed up for this. Sprout a pair of balls, bruv!"

An abrasive nudge coaxed Julien forth. Cautiously, he sank down the tarnished rungs of a rigid ladder. Fluidity of the motion lapsed under his up-skirt view. The sight of Blair's supple buttocks in periwinkle lace panties caused him to crash to the bottom.

Scrawny backside hitting dirt, Julien glimpsed Blair's final steps as his eyes roamed higher. Stalactites garnished the roof of what resembled a dungeon. Coal gargoyle statues were perched on oil lamps, orange flames wildly flickering at their talons. Ladybugs crawled into their snarling mouths, bashful.

"A clumsy cameraman and ya creepin' skills are rubbish."

The taunt's impact was softened by Blair entwining one of her arms with Julien's, assisting him in standing. The prickly bristles of a broom brushed centipedes off his back pockets, puppeteered in midair. Noah, sliding out of a shadow, whistled for recognition of the deed.

"So happy for yi to join us. Now, Piper can get on with her lecture," he stated, pointing ahead to a boulder where Father Nigel and Tatyana stood.

Playfully skipping around the enormous, fungi-wrapped rock was a diminutive petite girl, clad in a peewee variant of Blair's uniform. Alopecia gouged patches into her frizzy auburn hair. Severe eczema encrusted her clenched fists. Despite obvious ailments, the girl was more chipper than a puppy fetching a tennis ball for the first time. She energetically waved at the two newcomers, asking that they wish her good luck. Her voice, airy with a thicker Geordie accent than Noah's, cued Father Nigel.

"Welcome to your first lecture. This one will be a double-decker, since Piper will be having a test. She belonged to the same class that Victoria did and is a crucial resource to you both, having fought the Oath Keepers. Please, don't be afraid to open your books and ask questions!"

"What do you mean when you say *class?*" asked Julien.

Piper headbutted the boulder, debris nuggets scattering. She sneezed, dust clogging her nostrils.

"That's what envoys call the Elehominum that help the Celortus. Me and Noah are glad to have yi as our replacement classmates!"

Julien and Blair had seen a myriad of darkly marvelous spectacles in their infantile stint at Edenshire Academy, but were left aghast at Piper's demonstration. Unscathed, she sniffled and gathered pebbles, audibly counting. Four eyes darting from her to Father Nigel, they saw him adjust his left sleeve. An exact copy of the bracelet that Tatyana flaunted during the Preux family interview, wolf head charm included, constricted his wrist.

"Tatyana wore that same bracelet when I first met her. Now, I see the priest with one. Does it symbolize something?" questioned Julien.

Piper massaged the rocky bits into daggers. "The Celortus make those for envoys. They're kinda like tracking devices, helps them find us and the school."

Gliding in the middle of the enchanted congregation, Noah lounged on purple fog. Julien and Blair surveyed the spectral chair, noting its horned armrests and legs. He sat reposed, spectating. Their stares, blatant and unyielding, earned them their own seats. Contorted erections of hazy skulls elevated them, generous offers from Noah's ectoplasm.

A bird's-eye view was perfect for analyzing the scene. Piper, on her hands and knees, wove a gravel boomerang. Her crafting was intricate, mini dots furnishing the wings.

"I beg your pardon," grumbled Father Nigel. "Julien asked what do the bracelets symbolize. You should have informed him that the charm is an ode to the original protectors of the Celortus: wolves."

Noah's sinister puppetry at Blythe Gardens turned wolves into monsters. The nefarious fiend that hunted Julien and Blair was a far cry from protector. The truth of fact and fiction were muddled by his magical joke. Piper's bowed head, however, confirmed their nobility.

Father Nigel stroked his beard. Behind him, Tatyana pawed into the soil, slowly extracting a beige instrument one inch at a time. Brandishing a swiveled sword made of bone, she twirled it. The blade sliced through the air.

"Orphans encased in a manger, wolves secured them from danger. Delivered from the jaws of a jaguar and into the homes of kind shepherds, near and afar," the priest sang, along with Noah.

"That poetic ballad is not a jingle but a historical ark for the Celortus," said Father Nigel. "Inside the meters are biographical anecdotes that Ms. Woolgar should have known to quote to the letter. Her forgetfulness cannot go unchecked."

Dashing, Tatyana took a downhill swipe at Piper. Horrified, Julien and Blair protested the barbaric punishment, cursing Father Nigel. They leapt to sprints, hellbent on rescue, but small sinkholes subdued them. Synchronized with their foiled run was Piper's evasion. She cartwheeled, preventing a laceration.

Ghostly hands plucked the would-be saviors up, jerking them back into their seats.

"No cheating on tests," Noah chastised. "She's graced by terra firma and believe you me, the twerp can fend for herself!"

Blair threw up her arms in frustration. "And what the hell is terra firma?"

"Means she's handy with rocks and dirt," clarified Julien. "I learned that term in a geography lesson."

"Yee, that's reet, mate. Best I've ever seen do it, she is."

Noah's confidence in Piper's earth-centric power did not placate Julien and Blair. Grudgingly, they sat on pins, spectators in a blood sport.

Three stone daggers were tossed at Tatyana's chest, each one narrowly parried. The nun ducked the initial two and swatted the third to the left. No taller than waist-level, Piper squared off against her opponent. Unflinching, her breathing was relaxed.

"What is the only way to know the fullest extent of yi grace?" asked Noah, his voice echoing.

The testing format was clear. With every question, a verbal and combative answer had to be provided.

Pointed sword thrusts alternated between high and low, nicking blue polyester fabric. One miscalculation and Piper's organs would burst free. Julien sweated, fearful that he had a front-row ticket to a catastrophe.

Stone-faced, Piper blocked Tatyana from stabbing her with the aid of that boomerang. Evading, she hacked at the nun's shins.

"Our grace grows with us. The more that we study and train, the stronger they're ganna become. That's why we've got tests."

Father Nigel cocked one of his trusty nine-millimeter pistols and everyone froze. He strutted toward the standstill melee and examined both young ladies for facial swelling. Thumbs detecting none, he smiled and stepped back, letting them have a moment.

Weapons relinquished, they hugged. Tatyana rested her chin upon one of Piper's bald spots, embracing her how a mother would her only daughter. Short, wiry arms returned the affection, squeezing tightly. Separating, they stood at attention and listened for Father Nigel's address.

"The relationship between Elehominum and envoys is one of tough love," he professed. "We must prepare you for unadulterated strife. Firstly, this technique may appear ruthless to you, but know that we would forfeit our lives to save yours. 'Tis the Wolven way."

"Look, I've seen mock voodoo rituals in Haiti and even they weren't on par with what's happening here," said Julien. "I like folktales and traditions, but I'm not sure I understand what you're talking about. Can you explain stuff a little more clearly?"

"You're rambling in riddles. We don't even know what the Wolven way is supposed to be," Blair added.

"Chivvy along to the Library of Solstice," Father Nigel said to Piper. "Tutor until brunch. Should you be uncertain of anything, save the questions and I will answer them when we reconvene."

Humming, Piper skipped to the ladder. Julien and Blair were unsure how she could shift gears so quickly. One second, she was a pint-sized gladiator and the next, an adorable darling.

"Not me best showing but progress is a slow process," Piper admitted. "We spar to keep on the up and up. Bit rough for learning, sure, but helps us not to fold under pressure. C'mon, I'll show you guys where to read more about it."

Blair threw a practice jab. "Sparrin' is for UFC fighters. I ain't have no fancy gyms when I was learnin' how to scrap. My cancer treatments are what taught me to never give up. Definitely lookin' forward to see-in' how I fare."

A series of click-clacks rang off the ladder's steps, each of the Elehominum scaling. Midway to the top, Piper shook her head up and down.

"Yep, but you won't have as much time as Noah and me to get better. Just gotta learn fast is all. I know you'll be awesome!"

The glee in Piper's affirmations was encouraging. She knew nothing of Julien and Blair but saw potential in them. The speed at which they would have to realize it, though, was concerning.

"Victoria and the Oath Keepers are coming. The bracelets heat up when Elehominum are close to an envoy. Father Nigel and Sister Agnieszka said they've never been this hot before," explained Noah, the last out of the skyward hole.

Fed a surplus of lies, Julien did not understand the nun's need for a pseudonym. He was beginning to distrust her, skeptical of her enigmatic policies.

"I thought her name was Tatyana?"

A cold pat on the back from Noah almost sent Julien stumbling to the depths. Posturing up, he avoided a critical injury. His right penny loafer was scuffed on the edge of the grandmother clock, an ugly blotch stripping its paint.

Noah laughed. "That's just one of her aliases, mate. See, I'm not the only one pulling tricks!"

"Sorry, he can be cheeky," apologized Piper, tweaking Noah's nipple between her index finger and thumb. "Joking cures his depression. He thinks stuff's funny when it isn't. He means well, though."

Noah yelped when she pinched him, the ashen skin under his shirt undoubtedly bruised.

"Edenshire Academy always has two envoys, usu-
ally a man and a woman. That's so the school can be
ran by one, while the other watches the outside world.
Sister Agnieszka's who does the scoping. She's got a
lotta enemies, so she wears disguises," Piper revealed.

"Never considered myself to be a feminist cuz I
don't mind preferential treatment. Boys that like pretty girls are the easiest to rob. They're too busy playin'
pocket pool to notice their wallet's been jacked," said
Blair. "Gotta admit that I'm diggin' Sister Agnieszka's
swag."

"Yeah, other than the Oath Keepers, who would
be dumb enough to try her?" Julien asked.

"The Oath Keepers just want the Celortus," said
Piper. "Sister Agnieszka was part of a nun covenant
in Warsaw that hunted witches. They ripped their
skeletons out and shelved 'em as trophies. Those who
escaped promised to get revenge."

Julien stopped, his gut rattling in revulsion. He
had no affinity for the religious, but could not picture
them executing in their God's name. Atheism kept
him ignorant to the Old Testament's violent obscen-
ities.

Then it clicked in his head. Piper dodged a mar-
row machete.

"So, that thing she was trying to stab you with..."

Noah wiggled his arms and puckered. "Yep, belonged to a goat-sacrificing wench!"

Mutely, Julien tried to discern if Sister Agnieszka's
previous alliance was just, his legs on auto-pilot.

The Elehominum whipped around the staircase where an elevator awaited. A discolored tablet decorated slanted iron gates, Roman numerals one through four etched on it. Pressing the third button on the panel, Noah ushered everyone onto the grass rug inside.

Leisurely, the elevator clinked. Blair and Piper candidly conversed about the duel with Sister Agnieszka, commending her fencing. Their blooming friendship left Julien seemingly forgotten. He sulked, watching them whisper and joke. A nebulous breeze fluttered the older girl's dress. Noah winked at him.

"Her bum is lush," Noah murmured to Julien, directing the group out of their sardine can and into a mint green chamber once the elevator doors squeaked open.

Bamboo columns stretched infinitely, shelving books that varied in width. Rose petals were sprinkled along the top edging.

"Everything written by old Elehominum and their envoys is in the Library of Solstice. It's all here, from how to get more in tune with your grace, to what weakens it, to our feud with the Mavkardia," Piper informed, trekking enthusiastically. "I love the poems we have on retirees, but yi might find something yi like better."

Blair kept pace, blue veins flexing in her calves. Strawberry blonde locks bobbing, she opened her mouth to ask a question, but the walking cheat sheet next to her had other plans.

Piper, ever the livewire, skipped ahead. Loafer heels bounced her over pink eraser shavings on the concrete. She decelerated at the foot of a lumber table. Blair, the lone student to chase after her, stopped in time to avoid a collision.

"Old? I was under the impression that this was permanent. Are ya tellin' me we won't always have these powers?" asked Blair.

"Correct, pet," said Noah, Julien at his side. "If yi die, natural or otherwise, your body will release the grace during rigor mortis, and it'll become free to bond with someone else. Or, you can ritualistically forgo it to the Celortus. Piper's mam did when she was born."

Blistered hands sorted through rows as the little girl stooped, plucking a book composed of decaying leaves from its holding place. Carefully, she flipped to a photograph of a burly Amazon whose quadriceps were mountainous. An ash stripe was on her forehead. It was war paint.

"She fought for them, ill and pregnant. On my birthday, ten years an Elehominum, she surrendered her power to the Celortus. It's been tough doing her old grace justice, but she never stops encouraging me. That's me mam: Ellis Woolgar, the saint."

Piper's admiration of her mother called for a minute of silence. She was legendary, boasting a decade-long résumé of mettle. Wrought with emotion, the second-generation Elehominum sniffled, clutching the book to her bosom.

Clapping, Noah broke the silence. "We've got a geet walla history, us Elehominum. Do some shopping and let's meet back here!"

Dispersing, the four roamed the silent domain unchaperoned. Stapled papers piled high on azure blue trays, alphabetizing authors and genres. A universe all its own, the library was dense with lore that begged to be read. No sector was visited by the same children.

Non-fiction novel manuscripts lay atop olden day typewriters, glass-cased relics tucked beyond the earliest entry points. Sapphire ceiling lamps discouraged touching, flashing upon detecting heartbeats. Weary of the alarm, Julien elected to skim the selection of magazines on a wall-mounted rack. Uniformity in cover art did not allow for much creativity. The template was rudimentary: a tertiary color background, centered listing of staff members, publication date, and, in underlined print, the title.

Eyes shut, he blindly chose the exclusive cyan issue. Its texture was sleek, unlike the matte others his fingers plunked. Squinting, he read and walked.

"Elehominum graced by ectoplasm, better known as 'Grimemories', are not devils. On the contrary, they are lighthearted and selfless. Their sullen talents are for envoys needing council with lamented predecessors."

Julien meandered, analyzing his classmate's off-putting personality.

"That kid does seem demented and perverse, but my parents taught me not to judge," he mumbled, thinking of Noah. "Probably was hard for him hearing Piper talk about her mom, too. I couldn't imagine being an orphan. I'm sure he's got some good in him."

Backtracking to the meeting place, Julien pondered the feasibility of him contacting Jean-Renee. He had no clue what the properties of ectoplasm were, nor its restraints but would resent himself for not asking.

Repeated U-turns came to a closure. Seated with their faces glued to blocks of text, the graced children did not acknowledge when he rejoined them. They had become bookworms, reading themselves into solitary confinement. A broken-legged chair scraping against concrete ended their serene concentration.

Scooting next to Noah, Julien ignored the impolite stares. "I'm not really sure how to go about this so I'll just ask: can you please use your ectoplasm to help me talk to my great-grandfather?"

"No, he cannot! The graces are our gifts, not some spiritual phoning service to make calls with. Have you gone mad, like?" an irate Piper rebuked, slamming her book closed.

Gasping, Julien hadn't anticipated such a vehement resistance to come from Piper. His petition, naive and pompous, was grounds for her to disregard the age hierarchy that schoolchildren universally adhered to. Brows arched, Blair pondered the severity of ectoplasm's trivial usage. The periodical she busied herself with criticized immodest practices, gratuitous enactment of graces ranking chief.

Illustrating comic strips of them in morgues, Noah could not help but snicker. "Now, now! I'd be doing a favor for a friend. No one has to know what's happening," he said, digging out a titanium locket from behind his shirt's buttons.

Piper glared at the shiny octagonal trinket. Her eyes shifted from its center screw to Blair, pleading for backup.

"I'd like to see it, if I'm honest," admitted Blair.

Disappointed, Piper's head fell in shame. She slouched and sighed.

"Three to one? I do believe that means we've outvoted yi, lovely," taunted Noah, sticking his tongue out at her.

Piper snubbed the heckles, glaring at him. Patchy legs swinging under the table, she tried to cave in his kneecaps.

Life was hard for smaller children. They were talked over or went unseen in groups, eclipsed by their taller peers. Julien saw countless bullies target the weak at Frederick Douglass Junior High, physically harassing them and defecating in their book bags. He was briefly sympathetic, guilt-ridden that his impulse conflicted with patriotism.

Remorse for Piper's discontent was soon forgotten, its memory replaced with occult wonders. Everyone was fixated on the sodium chloride that pooled from Noah's locket. He churned the screw, prying into the inner recess to expel more until it inexplicably and loudly slammed shut.

"Salt keeps the bad spirits at bay," Noah informed. "You open a portal and anyone can come through. Some are pleasant, some are dastardly. I've learned to use my discretion."

The young mastermind was fast at work, meticulously arranging the colorless grains to form a pentagram. A perfectionist, he measured points for consistency. The straightness of the borders was immaculate, even impressing Piper, who was too angered to speak.

"Spit," said Noah, elbowing Julien.

"Huh?"

"Mate, spit in the salt and say his name. You have to make a peace offering to the spirit. If he's your great-grandad, he'll recognize your DNA and be more likely to talk."

The commandment was gross to Julien. Slobbering was the last thing he wanted to do in front of Blair, fearing she would think he looked like a blithering idiot with his rank tongue slipping past his protruding lips. She stared at him from across the table, anxious to see a black miracle.

A pathetic spitball dribbled, the prelude to Jean-Renee's name being spoken. Noah kneaded the mixture, widening the five-pointed star.

"We'll now stand and join hands."

Defiantly, Piper remained seated, gritting her teeth. She was scolded by the others, who ridiculed her for being stubborn. Caving to peer pressure, her arid fingers linked with Julien and Blair's.

Head snapping back, Noah breathed deeply and the séance commenced. "From whence this humble contribution has come, I call upon the Five Truths of Refinement: conviction, cunning, desire, melancholia, and zeal. Transform my body into a vessel so that the unreachable gateways may be tangible."

His eyes dilated, lids inverting. Shivering, chill bumps daubed his neck. Uneven ropes of thorny ectoplasm shot out of his mouth, producing a gurgling noise.

Wonderstruck, three hearts thudded in unison. Their grips tightened. The pentagram then slanted toward Julien. Petrified, they gulped as the purple matter Noah spewed took the shape of a man.

"I worry that you have inherited my son's audacity; disturbing eternal rest is rude, even when it is done by your great-grandson!"

The quip, delivered by an accent cooked in a Haitian and English melting pot, authenticated the existence of ghosts. Stuttering, Julien was inundated with meeting the Preux patriarch, albeit in a less-than-flattering state. A wispy silhouette did not mirror the ebony man he saw in his dreams.

"How do I know this isn't a hoax," he asked. "Prove that I'm actually talking to Jean-Renee!"

The apparition's shadowy arms were shaken exasperatedly.

"You've woken me up and I have to prove who I am? Even when I have popped my clogs, this family doesn't respect me," Jean-Renee complained. "Let's see: your grandfather, who is my son, is named David and his brother is Daniel. Your father is deathly afraid of chickens."

"I wasn't trying to be disrespectful, it's just that Noah's known for pranking folks," explained Julien, swelling with pride. "My twelfth birthday wish was that we'd meet somehow. I never stopped believing in the stories about you and alchemy, not even when my dad tried his hardest to make me."

"I would have enjoyed conversing with a Preux who doesn't think I'm a liar. This meeting may not be idealistic but, we have an allotted time frame to be spent intelligently."

A sense of urgency arose. Julien could not shower Jean-Renee with adoration or analyses of his work.

"Your notepad has been preserved, but I haven't solved for the variables. Was that formula how you figured out the mechanics of transmutation?"

"Those are not variables. They are heirlooms; the archived initials of our family members who fought in the Haitian Revolution. The numbers beside them represent the total of Frenchmen they killed during the insurrection, from 1791 to 1804," Jean-Renee construed.

Julien remembered reading snippets about that violent uprising in his World Politics course. A successful anti-slavery coup d'état demolished the white supremacy narrative. Colonists were lynched and beheaded, evicted for the sake of democratic independence. The massacres gave Haiti sovereignty, an inalienable victory. Tracing his lineage to a crucial segment in history left him flabbergasted. His great-grandfather's writings were blood-soaked memoirs, not an alchemical blueprint.

"If those are just casualty details, how did you make gold?" he asked.

"Alchemy is the science of sacrifice, a seesaw of creation and destruction," he explained. "During thunderstorms, I cut myself and bled 80 times onto cinnabar ores, equaling mercury's atomic number for a union of man and material. My O negative blood then destabilized the mercury, activating beta-plus decay to remove one proton. Gold only has 79."

Julien knew that the process Jean-Renee disclosed, removal of a proton from a nucleus, required a nuclear reaction. Abominable was a fitting description for his method. He mutilated himself in exchange for treasure, a gravely trade.

"I experimented with pain, assuming the endorphin release would be an adequate swap," he continued. "It wasn't 'til I met an Egyptian philosopher at a fruit marketplace that I learned to suffer smartly. He gave me a pyramid shard from the Nile's belly, and inscribed on it were the precise conditions of transmutation."

"But at the cost of your own well-being? Anything

that endangers health to that degree is no good," Julien rationalized.

"God, in my assumption, would deliver us from despair but our prayers went unanswered. I renounced Catholicism after I tired of seeing my relatives and friends scrape scraps of rice and overripe plantains. Their livelihood was worth my torture. I regret nothing."

Julien, born with a silver spoon in his mouth, knew not the horrors of destitution. Clean water and disease vaccines were delusions for the penniless, their lives devoid of bare necessities. Had it not been for his great-grandfather's monetary masochism, he, too, would have drunk from desecrated rivers, desensitized to droughts, famine, and brutality.

The smog projection that reanimated Jean-Renee began to fizzle. A gradual disappearing act, puffs ate him down the middle. Short-lived was that generational summit.

"I'm afraid our time has come to an end, pitit gason mwen," he bemoaned. "I leave you with one piece of advice: trust in yourself. The genes of Hispaniola impel you to fight oppression. Do not fear losing; fear not trying. M'swete'w tout bon bagay."

"M'ap fe tout efo pou mwen apran."

Some untapped half of Julien spoke that last phrase, fluent in Kreyòl, just as Jean-Renee had withered to a huff of evanescence.

Slurping up the remnants of ectoplasm, Noah burped. "Worse than indigestion, I tell yi, man! Those answers better be up to snuff because my tonsils and lungs are throbbing. Won't be in a state to channel spirits anytime soon."

"Your grace has restrictions?" questioned Blair.

"They all do. You'll have to figure out what yours are by researching here. If I can't breathe properly, my talents won't work. Constant moisture hinders what Piper can do."

"Reet, which is why the graces should be conserved," Piper claimed. "Victoria and the Oath Keepers aren't kidding around. If we aren't ready when they come, they're ganna kill us."

Her eyes drifted to Julien, who gaveled his balled fist onto the table, shattering it. "Enough of this pessimism. We will be ready. I can promise you that!"

Sister Agnieszka's guttural Polish cadence rang throughout the Library of Solstice, shouting directions to the mess hall. Brunch was ready.

CHAPTER V

The random desire to be a leader spurred Julien henceforth, navigating for the Elehominum. He listened to Sister Agnieszka, a human GPS, who gave the exact coordinates of their next destination. She predicted it would take them four minutes and thirteen seconds to reach Edenshire Academy's dining quarter.

Lifted in that artifact of an elevator, they emerged before a tunnel on the third floor. Lanterns dangled over the gap, radiance shining.

"It's just up ahead. I'm positive yi can smell the cooking from there," said Piper, walking behind Julien.

Diverse aromas suffused, calling to the Elehominum's famished stomachs. Father Nigel and Sister Agnieszka welcomed them at the passage's entryway, distributing opal chalices as they entered.

"Real different from the cups I sip whiskey and coke out of," commented Blair, ogling the coiled handles. "Makes me think of Game of Thrones and King Arthur."

Lean-cut meats filled frying pans that sat on top of a flowery tablecloth. To the right of each were plastic containers, packed to the brim with hard-boiled eggs, fresh fruit, and leafy green vegetables. Jugs, two of water and the others of prune juice and soy milk, were spread along the table's four corners. Saucer plates and silverware were stacked in front. It was a health nut's version of a feast.

One after another, the children picked their food before settling onto onyx thrones. Father Nigel, the last to be seated, then sermonized.

"For those who wish to partake, I will lead us in a Catholic meal prayer. There is no onus to join in if you are not compelled. I ask that all of you, out of deference, refrain from eating 'til the prayer is finished."

Piper sat to the immediate left of Julien. The spinach chips, celery sticks, diced cucumbers, and lettuce on her plate were loyal to a vegetarian diet. Hands folded, she did not lay a finger on anything before the formal intercession.

Noah was already cutting into a chicken breast.

"Bless us, O Lord, and these thy gifts, which we are about to receive from thy bounty, through Christ our Lord. Amen," recited Father Nigel with support from Piper and Sister Agnieszka.

"Let us also give thanks to our God, who rules in Heaven, on behalf of those that do not share our beliefs. Be they non-believers or Agnostics, it is He who has supplied us with this daily bread," stated Sister Agnieszka.

"Aye, even if one of 'em is the lovechild of Satan's loins," Piper snarled, eyeing Noah.

"Rather be that than some rock-headed hacky slag who was baptized in the Tyne's water!"

Father Nigel dinged a spork on the rim of his chalice. "Ms. Woolgar and Mr. Satterly, I tire of you behaving like spiteful ruffians. You're two of Edenshire Academy's finest and I will not say it again: cease this buffoonery or you will be handcuffed together. Impolite remarks have no place at a mess hall brunch!"

Their grumbled insults abated, weakened by that ultimatum. Julien snickered, shoveling lightly seasoned sirloin steak and broccoli into his mouth. The exchange of insults between the youngest of the bunch were comedic brilliance to him.

"Mr. Preux, may I have a word with you," requested Father Nigel, calmly departing with a dark brown, beaded blanket folded under his left arm.

Chewing a mouthful of lamb meat, Blair's green eyes tracked Julien's movement past replica maces that were stuck to the lilac walls.

"In every class, there is one Elehominum who the others look to for strength. Us envoys have a knack for knowing who it'll be early on," Father Nigel said. "You're the trailblazer. Piper and Noah may currently be more adept with their graces than you, but they are young and impressionable. Set an example that does not encourage stupidity."

Lectured like he was the oldest of two misbehaving siblings, Julien stood beside the mess hall's entrance. His head was lowered in embarrassment.

"I'm sorry, I didn't think a few laughs would be a problem."

"Lad, you've misunderstood me. We want you to enjoy yourselves in the downtime you have but make no mistake, altercations need to be avoided. Peace-keeping is a prerequisite of being a leader. Sister Agnieszka and I are here to teach, not babysit. You have to learn how to keep them content yet focused, or they won't see you as fit. To do that, you must master your grace."

Father Nigel's critique baffled Julien.

"I was almost blown to smithereens in a plane crash. Why do you assume a snap of your fingers is going to turn me, a 15-year-old nerd, into the commander of a group of magical children? It's preposterous. What makes you so sure I won't have a change of heart, and decide this isn't for me?"

"The toughest challenges are those battled internally, in the solitude of our minds, those that keep us awake in the wee hours of the night. The ease of quitting will be a nonstop enticement, but it can be quieted. I have something for you."

Pinching the blanket by a bead, Father Nigel unveiled a platinum tome that gleamed vivaciously at Julien. Glossy, creased pages turned independently and created metallic clangs. Levitating, it zoomed upward and raced laps across the ceiling.

"Hey, you never said there'd be flying books!"

Perfectly timed with Julien's panicked avowal, the shiny book dive-bombed and burrowed its way underneath his loafers to lift him.

"Do not hold it against me. This is a learning experience and if I told you every detail, there would be no incentive for you to grow," Father Nigel reasoned. "Also, you might have known, had you been studying in the Library of Solstice instead of clarting about, and having Noah contact your great-grandfather. Consider it poetic justice."

"Yeah, about that. I, um," stammered Julien, weary of plunging head-first onto a rusty tack.

"You now have a study tool that will demand your cooperation and collaboration. You may simply think it a flying book, some novelty toy infused with magic, but I will testify to its majesty: the Mantrametalicus is a masterpiece of priceless caliber," Father Nigel proclaimed, backpedaling into the mess hall.

Julien's shaky legs began to steady. The book was stationary, suspended a foot in the air, which made him presume descending mount would not be difficult. Angling himself onto the balls of his feet, he grabbed the top intersections. Their icy feel sent a shiver up to his larynx. Molars loudly chattering, he did not notice the glittery, hooked apparatus that crystallized behind him.

Suddenly, the room was drained of color. Whiteness wholly camouflaged the interior, leaving only the glare from the lantern tapestry. All warmth waned.

Julien was jerked upslope. "I can't catch a break."

Hugging the underside of the Mantrametalicus for dear life, his tonsils quivered from screeches. Loop-the-loop transit curdled his digestive tract, but barfing had to be put on the backburner. Spontaneous wall surfing necessitated his undivided attention.

Accelerated speeds spun Julien around in a twister. Rotund lips madly flapping, his right arm rose and latched onto what he could now clearly see was a hook. Legs flailing off the ends of that interim surfboard, he was stumped on how the other affiliates of the secret society he had pledged to had not discerned his distress. Unquestionably, if they did, he thought, all five would have liberated him from that non-consensual joyride. Deliverance came not by their doing but by way of magnetic attraction that tugged him through the deck.

The fall had no booms or crackles. Yellow-green shapes haphazardly glistened over yonder, distant in the plummet. Color, regardless of its shade, was a welcomed change from the smothering white.

Plopping with a bounce, Julien was dumbstruck by his lower extremities remaining intact, despite the sheer drop from which he fell. Standing, he paid no mind to the insignificant cramp in his tailbone. The wormhole he sunk into unreservedly engrossed him, for it was a chrome clone of the Library of Solstice.

"Talk about celebrity makeovers. This place didn't look half as awesome the first time I was in here," he rambled, unaware of the book rotating above his head.

Cascading, the Mantrametalicus nestled in Julien's clasp, heavy and cold to the touch. Embroidered on the front was an inverted ankh. Its pages flittered, stopping on a page bordered by snapshots of a man whose pigmentation was bounteous in melanin. His woolly hair was styled into an afro, and an imperial mustache gave him whiskers.

"That's because you hadn't yet possessed the Mantrametalicus, my boy. There are districts within the Library of Solstice exclusive to Elehominum who have their pass. Here, only those graced by metal and so fortunate to hold the treasure may enter. Bravo!"

Jean-Renee's inflection gave life to one of the images, its jawline actively operating. Sleepy eyes locked onto Julien, sizing him up. His shuddering and hunched posture were not overlooked.

"Plant your feet and take a brace. You've made it this far because the element exerting your grace senses an unparalleled tenacity. Had it seen otherwise, the hook you clung to would have gone haywire, instinctively flinging you and piercing your kidneys."

"This surprise crap is getting old! You could've given me some sort of warning. It isn't every day that you finally see your great-grandfather, and he's yapping from a book's margins," an irate Julien shrieked.

"I can see the fiery Preux disposition in you. That is what defines us: an insatiable appetite to know," said Jean-Renee. "Let scholarship be your cardinal principle. Intelligence was of key importance to me when I stood in your shoes."

Bug-eyed, Julien's mind was blown. The man he idolized had been an Elehominum of yesteryear. Humbled to share his destiny, he strived to suppress the yearning to badger him with query after query, thinking it best to live in the moment. His curiosity, however, would not be silenced.

"Why could we only talk for a short while when Noah contacted you?"

"The séance was only a temporary link between the living world and the spirit world. As is the bidding of the Celortus, Goldevoires, who are the Elehominum graced by metal, have a fraction of their memory channeled into the Mantrametalicus when a new user is appointed. We assist by answering questions that an envoy cannot."

Millions of potential questions flooded Julien's headspace, but none were more pertinent than what rolled off his cotton-mouthed tongue. "How do I use my grace? It just pops out randomly."

"New Elehominum will have inadvertent reactions if they haven't mastered their grace. It must be internalized, believed to be as real as the functions of a ribcage."

"I hadn't known this was even possible yesterday. There has to be an easier way to go about what you're telling me to do."

"Julien, there is nothing *easy* about what you have become a part of. Forget the notion of shortcuts; you will, however, find that tools everywhere in this gamut of the Library of Solstice are helpful to your grace and spirit becoming one entity."

"Tools?"

"Go on, take a peek at them."

Turning 180 degrees, Julien's eyes set upon a laboratory. Conical flasks, goggles, mixing cylinders, and surgical tongs floated at nose-level. Geometric equations scintillated, light casting off the instruments. Marveling at the craftsmanship, he moved in for a closer inspection. They lacked even the most common of mass production defects.

"The supplies here are flawless because they exist in an alternate quantum state, marginally out of phase from Earth's normal reality," Julien affirmed. "This part of the Library of Solstice can't be reached by conventional means."

A round of applause came from Jean-Renee, the stainless-steel cufflinks of his burgundy blazer dinging on the penny bracelets he wore.

"My word! Your comprehension of physics is phenomenal. Only a devout student of alchemy could aptly articulate what the majority of the world thinks inconceivable."

Julien was uplifted by Jean-Renee's exaltation of his studies. He smiled, feeling that his great-grandfather had legitimized the numerous writings of early alchemists he interpreted. Charles's opinions that alchemy was purely a pseudoscience were invalidated.

"Explains why no one heard me during the whiteout; I accessed the schism in our latitude."

"Accurate again. The Mantrametalicus grants you unlimited admittance here," said Jean-Renee. "When you're ready to depart, raise it overhead and chant the full date of your birth backwards. I'd wager a guess, though, that you won't be off anytime soon. The opportunity to freely experiment with dependent variables under abnormal circumstances does not present itself often to those your age."

Fingertips dragging over decimals afloat, Julien beamed in excitement when the upside-down triangles that oscillated in rotation jumped. Laughing, he tickled round their circumferences, thoroughly entertained by the spectacle.

Jean-Renee cleared his throat. "If you'd be so kind to stop molesting the operators, I would like you to begin your inaugural undertaking. Remember: you are to be working, not romping about."

Refocused, Julien righted himself in front of a long tray that had materialized. Individually, the buoyant appliances descended upon that ethereal surface. He fastened the elastic goggle bands around the back of his head. The lenses provided optimum clarity.

"My ophthalmologist told me that I had 20/20 vision in April. Looking through these has me feeling like my vision's been blurry until today!"

"Yes, they are quite the enhancement from one's

natural eyesight and with good reason, too," Jean-Renee explained. "You will need to appropriately identify the test subjects at your disposal in order to wangle
the desired results of the upcoming experiment."

Inspired by the prospect of becoming the Preux
family's second alchemist, Julien wrenched the tongs
from their position on the tray. "Alright, no more
games. Let's do this."

On cue with his words, the Mantrametalicus gy-
rated and an ivory yarn basket seeped through its
seam, propelled by Jean-Renee's blown breaths. Sit-
uated on a bed of candytuft flowers was a jar that
constrained a throng of extinct amphibian vertebrae.
Fishy gases discharged from their charred remains
and out of the dull lid's many holes, loitering about
two grayish lumps that were reposed on it.

"Careful not to deface them," warned Jean-Renee,
evaluative of how tight Julien's clench was when ac-
cepting the delicate container. "The tiniest misstep
could obstruct your transmutation of those lithium
slabs to titanium."

"What's coming out of this jar's openings has to be
fossil fuels. If I remove its cap, the energy needed for
transmutation will be released. Won't be on a thun-
derstorm's scale but beggars can't be choosers," Julien
thought, depluming the lithium with the tongs and
unscrewing.

Raw bee pollen coated the jar's top. Tawny pellets
soiled Julien's pinky. The idea to wipe that finger onto
his corduroys was derailed by a recalling of the dream
he had featuring Jean-Renee, and an injured panther
chameleon. The serial massaging maneuvers that re-
paired its damages occurred inside a circle, focusing

the harnessed therapeutic energy in a complete 360. He put two and two together.

"Alchemy is the science of sacrifice. Lithium has an atomic number of three but titanium has 22," he postulated, leering at the billows that pervaded. "My great-grandfather exchanged a bodily fluid. Pretty sure I have to do the same."

Removing the goggles, Julien hurled them by the bands at the Mantrametalicus to be assimilated by the book. Unprotected from the airborne combustible geologic deposits of organic matter, his tear glands were promptly irritated. Withstanding intense burning sensations that spanned from cornea to iris, he drew identical circles around both eye sockets with the bee pollen. A watery layer of tears frothed.

Rickety hand reaching for a flask, he blinked and the sticky streams were on the brink of overflow. "19 droplets should be all I need to account for the missing protons. Just have to angle this thing to snag them."

Scarlet vessels inflamed Julien's eyes. He counted the tears splashing into the glassware. They puddled at the baseline. Tensing, his hand that held both hunks of lithium with tongs went limp, letting the smallest tumble to the floor. Tilting the flask, he glazed it with one gracious downpour.

A sizzling sound triggered a convulsion in the lithium. It skidded to and fro. Those ballistic movements stopped when a thick grease cocooned it.

"I don't recall reading anything that alluded to this happening," muttered Julien, continuously poking the buttery chunk.

His consecutive prodding chipped away goo, fragmenting clumps into specks. Rinsed of film, a lustrous gray brick covered with tiny spikes debuted. Its composition looked brittle, antithetical to the soft metal it superseded. Transmutation of lithium to titanium had been achieved.

Julien celebrated in triumph. He was consumed with happiness, distracting him from the crust build-up in his eyelashes. Hooting about how deluded the other Preux men were for discrediting Jean-Renee's alchemy, he did not register the lightheadedness that snuck up until a misguided step knocked the tongs loose from his grasp. Dizzily, he clambered to catch the remaining lithium in his cupped palms.

Mesmerized by profusely varying slate pigments that rimmed its perimeters, he identified with the susceptibility to evolution. Indistinguishable from his transition of egghead to esoteric recruit, he saw his reflection in the coiled median. Inebriated on fumes, his uninhibited thoughts deciphered the subliminal meaning of Jean-Renee's advice. Cradled like a snoozing infant, the lithium was transported to Julien's rib cage.

"It's real. I believe it, I believe in my grace," Julien avowed, his hands now duplicative of the lightweight metal.

The traumatized faces of the Celortus flashed in his memory bank.

"A masterful interpretation of the merger," congratulated Jean-Renee. "Having dominance over your grace will galvanize you to defend what source it is that animates them: the Celortus. Lithium, nonetheless, is the weakest of the Seven Metals of Combat."

"What are those? The Seven Metals of Combat, I mean."

"Represented by the symbol you saw in my note-pad and at my gravesite, lithium, titanium, copper, zinc, mercury, silver, and gold are your mechanisms of defense and offense. Each requires a larger power source to be activated and maintained."

"Okay, I get that but I haven't roughhoused, let alone brawled! What good is having these if I don't even know how to properly throw a jab?"

"Very few Elehominum are born fighters before bonding with their powers. Once he or she has, the grace will fight for them."

Julien gazed at his shimmering fists. Loosely curled, they soared in front of his face, turning ever so slightly toward him to draw both elbows inward to shelter vulnerable body parts. Knees relaxed, he spread his feet moderately more than shoulder width apart, balancing on their balls with the majority of his weight on his back leg.

Chin tucked to his chest, he speedily threw his left arm out and rotated his palm down. Optimal extension verified by a swoosh, he retracted it and defaulted to his original stance. Dumbfounded, he had not expected to become a boxer overnight but the art of combat was addictive. A multitude of jabs were thrown at fluctuating elevations, discontinuing only when he fatigued.

"You have tired yourself out. The grace of metal, not unlike its counterparts, must be wisely managed, lest you risk depletion. Tonight, pore over the Mantrametalicus for a syllabus that comprehensively lists hazardous antics and natural weaknesses," Jean-Renee informed.

Exhausted, Julien lolled, screwing the lid back

onto the jar. Curiously scrutinizing the contents, he contemplated what would be powerful enough to activate the strongest of the metals.

"If lithium is at the bottom of the totem pole, gold must be sitting on high. How am I supposed to find something capable of generating that much verve?"

"It is closer than you think, pitit gason mwen," Jean-Renee cryptically hinted. "Reunify with your class and the answer will be apparent."

Julien sighed, intellectually haggard. "I'm grateful you have faith in my ingenuity. I won't disappoint you."

"We were among the needy and uneducated. Us Preux men have exceeded all expectations our ancestors had for a better life. The next chapter in our saga will be authored by you. Seal this book and go forth to write."

Obeying Jean-Renee's orders, Julien closed the Mantrametalicus, hiked it up to a cleft hair follicle, and chanted the cipher that would permit his return to the Library of Solstice's common spheres. The room wobbled, that stannic tinge washing away. Defaulted to its normal appearance, sundry colors and fragile furniture were restored.

Afflicted with what felt like carsickness, Julien resisted vomiting by swallowing upcoming undigested protein from the luncheon. Doubled, he was oblivious to his audience prior to a stapler shooting at him.

"Have ya lost your marbles, cameraman? This is a library and some of us intend to use it for the right purposes, which do not include barkin' like an imbecile!"

Blair's disparaging slander fell on deaf ears. Quibbling about vocal moderation with a wannabe librarian was severely unappealing to Julien, specifically when the alternative involved glorifying the Mantrametalicus. He wanted to scrub off the surviving incrustation that blotched his eyebrows, and hail Jean-Renee's inclusion in kick-starting his acceptance of metal as a grace. A momentary distraction had overshadowed the book's eminence, plundering the limelight.

Halfway unrolled in the feisty belle's lap was a canary-yellow papyrus scroll. Iotas of lightning fervently orbited the upper tendril. Julien, tantalized by their bustle, regained a perpendicular pose.

"Wow, that's a cool-looking piece of parchment. Where'd you find it?"

"It's the Electromni," Blair explained. "Father Nigel gave it to me for quietin' Piper and Noah while you were gone. Their arguin' got them the luxury of washin' dishes. I'd say they've been at it for about as long as I've been here."

"He gave me this," Julien piped up, waving the Mantrametalicus. "I haven't read a lot, but my great-grandfather spoke to me from the pages and said if I can become one with my grace, it'll fight for me. I started to shadow-box and by the end of it, thought that I could take on the world."

Blair zeroed in on his last sentence, spotting the yeasty hoops around his eyes and those shining fists. "The Bisping surname has been ringin' bells in caged fightin' lately, perhaps I can be of some assistance to ya. I don't have any formal trainin', but I'm scrappy and can push a pace."

Julien watched her place the Electromni on a nearby bookshelf. "I know you want to see where my heart is, but my dad taught me that hitting women isn't something a man should do. Kind of feels like I'm being tugged in one direction by my morals, and in another by validation. Then again, how could I have a snowball's chance at rescuing humanity if I don't step out of my comfort zone?"

Blair indecently cracked her neck, smirking when the joints boisterously popped.

"I don't think a little friendly competition is wrong," an anxious Julien laughed, tossing the Mantrametalicus next to the Electromni.

Any easygoing he hoped for fizzled with a round-house kick to his sternum. Blair's attack was so grace-ful that the pirouetting of her leg was a blur. The brunt of it floored Julien. She sensed his frailty and went in for the kill, rearing her left foot up to slam the heel down in the manner of an axe sharpened for a heretic's execution.

Knuckles cut along fired staples, Julien wheezed. He lifted his head at the precise moment that a shoe came hunting for his right orbital. Rolling aslant, he scurried to find footing. Steadying himself against a carrel desk, he sidestepped an incoming knee from her and unleashed a flurry of chops that found their mark on her slender midsection.

Thrashed, Blair waddled, holding her contused ribs. Julien thought the blows would have convinced her to concede, but she was not done.

"Is that the best you've got?"

The unbending, staunch mentality Blair had proved her to be Julien's equal. Voltages circling her thighs, he prepared for a barrage of dermis-frying strikes, guards ascending. She pivoted to whip the leg she initially attacked with at his esophagus but it strayed from the warpath, misdirected into a spin that ended in a flump by the drumbeat of frantic footfall.

"Noah's ganna have a test," Piper broadcasted. "We have to get to Chillingham Forest before sundown; Father Nigel and Sister Agnieszka hate tardiness!"

Julien loosened his fists and scrubbed away the bee pollen rings, relieved that Blair relented.

"Don't think you're out of the woods, cameraman. I still want to see what you can really do," she grinned, extending her arm for him to do the gentlemanly thing.

Julien's chivalry was rewarded with a zap that tingled his sinuses.

CHAPTER VI

The hurried withdrawal afforded Julien and Blair a momentary view of Edenshire Academy's outer architecture. Built from plum bricks, the school was a small-scale basilica championed by an onion dome where a peregrine falcon alighted, monitoring them under the clouded blue twilight. The sea swayed behind it, rippling.

"Divvent fash yisel, she won't swoop doon and gobble yi," Piper claimed. "Rabbi Tov told us she protects a special bow and arrow."

Julien's repetitive peeks at the avian were the catalysts for the smaller Elehominum girl's statement. His prudence was not out of wildlife phobia; he wanted ample time to juke any runny excrement. Her citation of Father Nigel's precursor, however, urged him to inquire about the incidents that peaked with three homicides.

"I've been wondering something: how is it that, even though your old class had envoys, people ended up dying? Aren't they supposed to be our caregivers?" he asked, strolling past a boysenberry-bearing bush.

The forest ahead, laden with blackthorn trees and hanging vines, distracted Julien. Absentminded, Piper's grimace went unnoticed until Blair alerted him, whispering suggestions to be more tactful, but his crass commentary was disastrous.

"Rabbi Tov deserves a memorial for everything he's done," retorted a frustrated Piper. "If he wasn't bedridden from lupus, he would've fought off the Oath Keepers and protected Victoria, and Amelia and Abigail would be alive."

"Are those the names of your classmates that were murdered?" asked Blair.

Piper moped. "They were Welsh conjoined twins that almost bled to death during their separation. Amelia was graced by hail and Abigail, snow."

"Their graces were depleted in the ambush," Blair surmised.

"Na. The lot of us were swimming at Wuthering Lake. The Oath Keepers found Rabbi Tov's dorm and torched him and Abigail with a flamethrower. She had just washed blankets for him," Piper recounted, scathing. "They came back the next year, this time with Victoria. Me and Amelia got attacked on our way to the shops. We fought hard, but it was too many of 'em. Victoria drowned Amelia in a whirlpool and she was ganna do me in, too, before Father Nigel saved me."

Julien, invested in that barbarous retelling, was unconcerned with the landscape of the declivity that led them into Chillingham Forest. Slithering adders were ignored. Wasp nests went neglected, despite the scratching noises they emitted.

Blair fumed at the atrocities she heard, grinding her teeth.

"They'll pay," assured Julien.

"Yeah, what goes around comes around," Blair agreed, nodding.

Piper was quiet. She dawdled beside Julien, who slowed at a campfire where Sister Agnieszka fed kindling to coral flares.

"My apologies for Chillingham Forest being the site of tonight's test. Noah has a penchant for its plants and wildlife," apologized Father Nigel, pushing through a hedge of overgrown tobacco weeds.

No sooner than the priest hushed, a lynched body dunked lateral to Piper, dangling on a hardy branch. A noose-knotted fiber rope hanged the corpse, startling Blair to gasps. Her hysteria quelled after the littlest one in their group narrowed her eyes. It was a deranged shenanigan from the star Grimemory himself.

Noah threw his head back and convulsed with hilarity. The lasso that cinched his thin neck dematerialized in a purple puff. River dancing on air, he mocked Blair's dismay, insisting that it was a reparation for her judgment of his upbringing.

"Relax, dude. She wasn't trying to rag on your parents," Julien intervened. "You don't have to be so vindictive; we're on the same team."

The straightforward reprimanding silenced Noah, his face drooping as he debarked onto a tree stump. Father Nigel applauded, delighted with Julien's mediation.

"A fair warning to all who plan to attend this test: live rounds will be shot. For your welfare, we ask that you take a step back to avoid strays," stated Sister Agnieszka.

Collectively, Julien, Blair, and Piper heeded the

nun's words. The odd man out, Noah meekly hummed and stretched. Premeditated maneuvering positioned him two meters apart from Father Nigel. His ironically timed droning stopped the moment he saw the hammer of a Colt Python cock.

"He may be a bratty lil' punk, but we can't sit idle while he plays Russian roulette!"

Blair's apprehension was not seconded by Julien.

"Listen, I know this looks insane but there's a method to the madness. I learned a lot when the Mantrametalicus took me to a different part of the Library of Solstice. We just have to endure the hazing. If we don't, we'd be going against a molding process and could be risking millions of lives. I'm sorry, but it is what it is."

"Sister Agnieszka will give the introductory question. Afterwards, pupils are to shout their own questions for Noah to answer. Let us begin," announced Father Nigel, spinning the barrel of his gun.

Paged, the nun stuck a stick into the fire. "Are the Mavkardia and Oath Keepers the same?"

Sister Agnieszka pulled from the source material of the jeweled textbook that was found in the schoolhouse's bedrooms. Having merely skimmed his, Julien forgot how confusing the information could be at times. Nevertheless, his gratitude for the imminent clarification was unspoken, censored with a gunshot.

The bang of that revolver stunned three of the young and gifted, including Piper, who was accustomed to the strenuous proving grounds of their school. They feared a calamity but were mistaken. Noah, steadfast in the wake of a speeding bullet, disappeared in a soupy steam and reappeared beside Sister Agnieszka.

"No. Mavkardia is what you call the few people who are actually graced by darkness. They've existed since the element imploded, creating groups that brainwash others to serve them," he confidently answered. "The Oath Keepers are just one of those groups, but very dangerous."

Noah's vanishing agility both amazed and reassured his allies that he was proficient in the use of ectoplasm. Blair and Piper cheered for him, shouting encouragement and whistling. Julien refocused their attention to quizzing.

"The Mavkardia can't just be recruiting regular, run-of-the-mill folks, not if Victoria is an Elehominum. Is there something they specifically look for?"

Father Nigel, sniffing out the bison and Swiss cheese on Noah's breath, pinpointed his relocation and blasted twice. The foggy endowments of the magician hurriedly carted him to the gap between Blair and Piper.

"Depends on the particular group's founder. The Serpentine Sect, whose extermination predates the Oath Keepers by a few decades, was the brainchild of a forked tongue Mavkardia called Klara von Schlange. She exclusively chose cannibalistic Persian snake charmers to be her followers," Noah explicated.

"So, this ends when all of those Mavkardia wankers are toasted. How many do I need to electrocute?" seethed Blair.

Three bullets shot at Noah, Father Nigel skillfully holding the trigger with one hand and repeatedly striking the hammer with the other. His fanning turned the cylinder and hit the firing pin, which sent breakneck succession gunfire zooming past Blair and Piper. They winced from the air's reverberations, and missed the breeze that reestablished the vacancy that divided them.

"Not even the Mavkardia are the root of our problems; darkness is and will remain to be until it's purified. We've gotta find the person who has the soul that bears immortal light. If the first envoy's fragmented manifestos are to be taken literally, only their illumination will erase the element's negative influence," prophesied Noah, reappearing toe-to-toe with Father Nigel.

"That is downright moronic. We shouldn't have to go on some directionless expedition to meet who Noah's referring to. Why wouldn't they save everyone the hassle and show up? There's got to be more to this, some missing piece of the puzzle," theorized Julien.

His confidential monologue terminated with the winged onlooker stooping from her perch and soaring over Piper's head, flying toward the blossoming moon.

"Noah Satterly, Grainger Street's very own," Piper derided, choking back snivels. "I see Victoria in me sleep. It's the same thing every neet I shut me eyes: her drowning Amelia. Sometimes, I hear Rabbi Tov calling. He says I gotta make this reet. Can yi promise me that we'll avenge them?"

Sister Agnieszka interlinked her ten fingers and pressed them to her right breast. "Please forgive my shortcomings as an envoy. I, too, relive the heartbreak of fruitlessly pumping Amelia's chest lakeside. I remember the rotted seaweed, bitter on her taste buds while I tried to give her mouth-to-mouth resuscitation. No apology can sufficiently convey my regret."

Noah leaped, skating opposite quadruple shots that blitzed the stems off four acorns. A slimy, violet line trailed him to the crown of the tree at Father Nigel's rear. Steadied on one foot, he flipped and landed in the embers, purple gases extinguishing them.

"One of the worst memories I have is burying my mother and father. I couldn't even talk after their caskets had been closed. I carved up this Chelsea smile myself, on the off-chance I'd hear my own voice again. I started writing a sonnet for my parents the night I got to Edenshire Academy, to vent. Amelia gave me the courage to recite it. I can talk again because of her. Yi have my word: those numpty wazzocks will be slaughtered!"

The envoys smiled, rubbing their bracelets.

"Grimemories and Geodactyls have, historically, feuded in classes because they have vastly different temperaments but their cohesion has been instrumental in our victories. Indubitably, you will keep that tradition alive," praised Father Nigel, tucking his modified ten-shooter. "Prior to his test, Noah requested we go further into the forest and stargaze. Those who do not wish to come are permitted to return to the school and revise."

Fireflies swarmed, their bioluminescence a beacon for the sauntering participants. Julien, fascinated with the docile beetles, intended to plod behind Sister Agnieszka but Blair glommed onto his arm, rerouting his progression beneath a drapery of shriveled moss.

"What, don't want to be alone with the Celortus?" he grilled.

"Don't be daft, bruv," she gibed, surveilling the secluded institution from afar. "Could've sworn I saw a dwarf scrabble through one of the school's top-floor windows. We should investigate."

"Your mind's playing tricks on you, Blair. Think about it: we're in the middle of freaking nowhere. Call me cuckoo, but I can't imagine Cumberchester Heights being a hotspot for tourism. Why would anyone, especially a midget, be snooping?"

"It was a dwarf, dammit, and I haven't got a clue why but it's better to be safe than sorry, innit? Gut instincts don't lie. Mine are tellin' me to act."

Julien's shifty eyes glanced at the migrating Elehominum and envoys. He considered informing them about the suspected breach, but preferred not to set off false alarms.

"Potentially foiling the schemes of school supply looters isn't how I envisioned my summer. Don't say I never did you a favor."

The duo sprinted to evacuate the darkening hedgy terrain, their agile footwork slowing before a cobweb-plastered scaffold. Uncertain about whether or not the brass platform had previously been present, they used the evening's starlight to inspect for topical wheel marks, but yielded no conclusive findings.

"I wouldn't mind reconsiderin' if that wasn't open," Blair alleged, referencing the ajar overhanging window.

Gulping, Julien gripped the transoms and joggled them to appraise the framework's durability. "My dad paid some contractors to remodel our house, and they had one of these. I got to climb it, but they said to never have someone else climb with me if it was shaky, so let's be careful."

Blair acquiesced, watching his ascension and the eventual languid treads he made along the catwalk toward an unsecured slot. Mimicking him, she scaled to the top and hopped the guardrail.

"Guessin' it's good that I ain't heard you scream, but clear the threshold. I'm crossin' the plank."

Hurling herself inside, Blair crashed into Julien, who was sidetracked with sifting a strap-hinge scrapbook. That mismanaged stunt threw both teenagers beyond the black curtains of a canopy. Snuggled, they were pricked by disconnected thumbtacks implemented to pin belated additions.

"Sexy blokes," commented Blair, waggling onto her derriere to snatch a picture of two youthful British soldiers manning anti-tank rifles. "Chest hair is a turnoff but these gents could get away with it. Think they survived wartime without gettin' horribly disfigured?"

"Try friending them on Facebook," Julien recommended, pointing at the scribbly epithet taped to the baseline.

"Nigel M. Bradshaw and Samuel Tov, the Queen's sharpest marksmen," quoted a repulsed Blair, gagging.

Clothed in shredded battledress, the future envoys were timelessly commemorated on photographic film. Formerly brawny with a sharp jawline, Father Nigel was the poster boy for masculinity prior to entering priesthood.

"You'll be 16-years-old soon, right? Not much longer and you can legally marry your bae," Julien ribbed.

"Cameraman *and* comedian, aye? Perverted jokes are obviously your specialty," groused Blair, shoving him off the cashmere bedspread of that comfy mattress.

Julien fell, noticing the room's seared floorboards. "Holy cow, this is where it happened; Rabbi Tov and Abigail were burned here."

The bedchamber was expansive. A walk-in closet sat rightward of the laundry chute, crowded with padlocked cabinets. A vanity set, blackened by cinder residuum, took up most of its posterior space. Rosaries hung on the crackled walls. Consecrating the bygone tragedy, it was but minimally updated.

"Spooky bein' where somebody was burned alive," griped Blair, springing from a sunken indentation as she scoured the scrapbook's pages. "Pamphlet clippings about haunted churches ain't exactly calming, either, but Father Nigel is a fantastic poet."

"Seriously? Let me hear one," Julien said, standing.

"Underworld cretins hath run amok and not been policed. Tamer of unruly poltergeists, my authority was ratified by Jesus Christ. Beloved redeemer and friend to minister, pastor, and reverend, to obey him is to heal so his sobering hands may mend. In the destructive company of godless Sodomites and salivating vampires, the Lord's begotten son molded me anew with vinegary wine and torrid pliers. I shall fearlessly protect modest chapels and grandiose cathedrals from Djinn and troll, for I wish to see God's babies harvest the saintly knoll," read Blair.

"Wow, if Edgar Allan Poe was a lyrical preacher, that would be a dead ringer for one of his poems," Julien said, resting on a dilapidated stool.

"The comparison to a literary bigwig like Poe is humbling, but presently unimportant. To what do I owe the pleasure of having you invade my privacy?"

Father Nigel's unforeseen interrogation startled the teenagers. They did not expect to be caught red-handed trespassing, presuming stargazing was a tedious hobby. Plumb in the spherical doorway, he gnawed a Cavendish banana, hungry for an explanation.

"We ain't checkin' your room for nothin'. Honestly, we wanted to make sure everything was alright."

"Blair swears there was a break-in. I wasn't sold, but my aunt Anedie always says sharks kill unsuspecting fish."

"Your patrolling was ethical, Mr. Preux. I am happy that you are committed to securing Edenshire Academy's campus," he commended, finally entering the room. "Ms. Bisping's suspicions have piqued my curiosity. Envoys are not omniscient. Therefore, I cannot reaffirm nor deny. Howbeit, I invite you to recap the specifics."

"You, Piper, and Noah were passed the vantage point. Sister Agnieszka shooed a bullfrog and immediately, I got the uncanny feelin' I was bein' watched. When I turned around, I saw something with a small body climb through your window."

"I'm not picking up any unfamiliar smells and, if you were worried about the scaffold, it's an old antiquity," Father Nigel said, shutting the window. "To ease your worrying, Sister Agnieszka and I will dust for fingerprints. Rabbi Tov's obsessive vigilance has to be upheld."

Blair dusted off the scrapbook, lint wafting. "He must've been a real chum. Gutted we couldn't meet him."

Father Nigel walked toward the closet. Lofty cupboards hid him from view. Reemerging after the sounds of clicking combinations echoed, he held an oxidized British Army helmet.

"We were womanizing alcoholics. What we saw on the battlefield reshaped our worldly outlook. God-fearing men, amputated and malnourished, begged us to find religion. Sam and I were brothers, blooded by repentance."

"That's deep. I never had that type of friendship with nobody in Southwark. I ain't even have anybody to teach me how to do my makeup or nothin'," revealed Blair. "But why would the Celortus choose you and him to be envoys if you were sinners?"

"Redemption removes a sinful man's horns and exchanges them for a halo," Father Nigel averred. "Sam was psychic. He wowed Israeli rabbinical trainers that oversaw the orphanages he volunteered at with mindsight."

Julien, respectful of the eulogy, did not speak until there was an awkward silence. "Rabbi Tov seems like he was a great headmaster, but he wasn't our envoy. Please, tell us about how *you* became one."

"My live-in nurse oatmeal bathed me. I ate gingerbread cookies, timing her whilst she clipped and filed my ingrown toenails. A typical autumn Thursday," Father Nigel prefaced. "The witching hour brought abnormalities, namely the impermanent restoration of my vision. A storm started and I was chucked out of my hammock, a whirlwind ferrying me across the moonlit cityscape. I fainted and awoke backstroking in a glittery pond. Spiraling from caramel mountaintops, red wavelengths recapped my transformation from fornicator to priest. I heard the gospel of the Celortus, and it emphasized the importance of envoys. They sung Sam's praises and exhorted me to become his successor. My allegiance to the clergy would not allow refusal. I was ordained to liberate."

His illustrative retelling hyped Blair, her faith in the priest's precarious strategies thickening. "Rabbi Tov can rest easy. The Celortus chose the right man for the job."

"I am flattered, Ms. Bisping. Your charisma will be useful tomorrow. Lecturing is tiresome. It takes a real workhorse to teach Elehominum."

"Wha-what," stuttered Blair. "I'm no lecturer; I've got dyscalculia!"

"Nonsense. The Electromni is relevant documentation of one of the rarest graces, and has universal parables."

"I think she'd be exceptional," Julien lodged, nudging the soon-to-be instructor. "If all else fails, she can shock whoever disrupts."

"Mr. Preux and I are equally doubtless. Come, we will write your lesson plan in lieu of teatime."

Exiting the room, Blair walked in Father Nigel's shadow. They were engaged in a stimulating conversation of educational etiquette. The forbiddance of her profane vernacular entertained Julien. He didn't know what a "bellend" was, but thought the angry reaction she had to its banning was hysterical.

"Sister Agnieszka, Noah, and Piper should be returning pronto. I'll hit up the Library of Solstice and browse the Mantrametalicus for now," he said.

Similar to a dog ready for playtime, the shimmery tome scudded into the room, vigorously bouncing.

Julien petted the Mantrametalicus' fringe and straddled it. "Mom and Dad haven't gotten me that Japanese Akita they promised. You'll have to do."

Differing from the initial wild ride on the book, his departure was calm. Smooth sailing brought him overtop the scarred penthouse's arsenic palisades. Elegant dips curtailed at his meager dormitory's doorstep.

"I do my best work when I'm comfortable," Julien generalized, pinky signaling to his bed. "Couldn't hurt to unwind; I aced my online geometry and calculus midterms poolside. Aim for the pillow that isn't buffed."

The Mantrametalicus teetered and he sloped to the mattress, catching the shiny book as it drooped lifelessly. Unbolted, its first page was a thin sheet that blended pieces of the Seven Metals of Combat.

Hieroglyphs depicted the various stances of the grace's previous holders. Pictured in the cleaved squares were Sumo wrestlers, Muay Thai kickboxers, karate senpais, and others who practiced less easily identifiable arts.

"Hearken, the grace of metal is concentrated within predesignated appendages of Goldevoires, thriving where it may fluidly circulate. Allowing it to flow to other areas is adverse, as it subtracts from the intended area of strength," the crystalline centerpiece stated.

The next page had red drawings of corroded bodies. Mangled, their butchered chests were varnished with sepia rust streaks.

"Heat is an executioner, and prolonged exposure to severe temperatures will cause one to forego their control of bowels, and prematurely erode cartilage," a glassy footnote read, hypnotizing Julien.

Lost in thought, he imagined a cataclysmic wild-fire. Cyclone infernos barred him from the other Ele-hominum, who wept, crucified on a minefield that was furnished with the intestines of their envoys. The bleak, carbon monoxide-polluted stratosphere dumped a furnace that became his tomb. Shackled, he begged for his parents' forgiveness, baking like a dinner roast.

Acid raindrops pounded against the shutters, rein-vigorating Julien. Disturbed by the lucid savagery of his third eye's foresight, he buckled the Mantrametal-icus and crooned to the waterlogged drumming. Homesick, the far-flung crescent moon was reminis-cent of the eleventh wedding anniversary tattoos his mother and father got discounted in the Dominican Republic.

"If I were a parent, I would definitely want the truth," he said, slouching. "My decisions shouldn't hurt them."

Julien knew abductions were commonplace in Washington D.C. Law enforcement posted bulletins in the city's four quadrants, profiling disappearances. Nonprofits rallied, advocating that pimps, enablers of sexual offenses, should serve harsher imprisonment stints. Victimized families bawled at outreach and prevention meetings.

Endeavoring to prevent his parents' inauguration to that sad club, he grasped the handle of the lug-gage he abandoned. His intention was to mail them a handwritten confession, disclosing the events that followed his departure.

"It is unfathomable. Charles and Sandra will think

you're using drugs," opined Jean-Renee, cached pages muffling his voice.

"That may be so, but some form of closure is better than none. They're too good of people to just be left in the dark, depressed about their kid. You hurt yourself for your family's benefit. I'm doing this for mine," Julien contended, silencing his great-grandfather.

A ballpoint pen and a logbook were extracted from the lowest pouch of his luggage, and clustered lap-level.

"To the people I love the most," he began. *"I haven't been completely honest about my trip to Newcastle."*

Wordy chunks marked the paper, colored in blue ink. The dreamy prophetic visions of Jean-Renee were relayed, graphically describing his musculature and plentiful scars.

"His triceps and elbows were gashed. Same goes for his testicles. I'm not a coroner, but I'd say a crowbar was used. The curvy, rake-like trails on him make me think so."

Next, Charles' profound disavowal of the Preux myths was angrily refuted.

"I partially blame Dad's denial. He downplayed Jean-Renee, his own grandpa, whenever I mentioned alchemy. How could he live with himself, knowing that he disrespected our family's folklore? I had to clear his name. For me. For us."

An incisive breakdown of the environmental terrorism threatening Earth's sustainability climaxed Julien's letter.

"Meteorologists don't have a clue. Earth's elements are alive, and they exist through projected manifestations of kids. Their cohesiveness keeps the planet livable but not without trouble. There's a cult that wants to kill off our species and reform civilization the way they see fit. For eons, there have been people called 'Elehominum' who prevent Armageddon. They're empowered by the elements. That's why I was called to Edenshire Academy. Like my great-grandfather, I am an Elehominum graced by metal."

Julien tirelessly critiqued what he wrote, punctuating and shortening run-on sentences. Editing aloud, his progressively blunt verbiage coaxed him to soften the distressing blows of his *exposé*.

"I have no problem about my service going unsung. The world will probably never believe that the Elehominum are real. Protecting you is what matters to me, not a silly trophy. I love you dearly, and will do what I can to thank you for giving me life on September 14, 2002."

Authenticating the testimony, Julien signed with two angular dashes through the first letters in his name. The idiosyncratic trademark was a throwback to the ambitious attempt he made at longhand in kindergarten.

Emotionally sapped, his tired eyes longed for a moment's rest. He yawned, the weakening rainfall relaxing him. A nippy draft burdened him with shivers. Lazily wobbling, he reached to latch the sash but stiffened.

Below the increasingly starry sky was a costumed gnome. A raggedy olive trench coat stopped at its cloven hoofs, which were jelled in a blotchy fungus. Head canting, the crinkled lamb mask it wore seeped a dark broth.

"Well, I'll be darned. Blair wasn't kidding. I gotta warn everybody quick," said Julien, witnessing a violin materialize in the creature's fuzzy pincers.

The call to arms was waylaid. Tottery strings strummed a low-pitched song that lulled him to dreamland.

CHAPTER VII

A whiff of maple syrup-drizzled blueberry pancakes, vegan bacon, and spicy turkey sausage was the Wednesday wake-up call. The continual dinging of a Dutch handbell awakened Julien, his stomach grumbling with emptiness. Bundled with the Mantrametalicus in his covers, he disengaged from their scratchy coddle and rose. The totality of his uniform had withstood a midsummer night's dreamlike misadventure.

"I must have been zonked. Not getting a restful sleep has me tripping," he assessed, ignoring the dingy snowflakes that fell outside.

The tolling reverberated louder. Recognizing it as an indicator of tardiness, Julien drowsily staggered out of his room, derailing Noah's scurry.

"Howay, man, yi slowin' wi doon, like," Noah said, handing him a nectarine. "That'll have to do, if you're wanting some scran. Father Nigel wants us in the auditorium no later than ten past six."

"Oh, yeah, Blair's teaching today. I'm hoping she's warmed up to the idea of it. My mom had a few college buddies that interned at a conservatory in east Los Angeles. They resigned before lunchtime. Stage fright sucks," replied Julien, devouring the juicy peach.

"She'll survive, mate. I don't get the vibe that she's a quitter. These assumptions can wait, though. We're cutting it close."

Noah placed his hand on the small of Julien's back and exhaled. A sludgy, purple-tinted blob skyrocketed them to Edenshire Academy's fourth level. Debarking their ectoplasmic lift, the young men zipped along green and white checkered floors.

Venus flytraps, harbored in unglazed ceramic pots, were hung by gable chains. Pendulums, they wagged over heated tanks where scorpions dined on helpless lizards and moths.

"This floor's architect was either an outdoorsman or an insect collector," proclaimed Julien, passing a red carpenter ant farm.

"Wey aye! Elehominum graced by verdure pulled double-duty as landscapers. It's become praxis that only Synthetarians design this part of the school. Me and Amelia jokingly called them 'Cabbage Patch Kids' but we loved their contributions," informed Noah.

Julien raised an eyebrow. "So, why is it that our class doesn't have one?"

"A new user hasn't been chosen," Noah explained, braking at an underpass crowned with grapevines. "Classes typically have eight Elehominum, but the elements choose when they want to grace a person."

They followed earsplitting clangs. Earthworms tapered their footpath, squirming. Jumbo grasshoppers chirped, lining the passageway's rim. A kaleidoscopic blockage of butterflies scattered to reveal the inconspicuous venue.

A podium overlooked old, wooden desks upgraded with cushioned stools and basalt benches. Piper sat rearmost, annoyingly chomping sunflower seeds. Sister Agnieszka vaulted off a colossal beanstalk onto moist soil, welcoming Julien and Noah.

"There is no assigned seating," she informed. "But a projector will be the principal equipment of this discourse. Please consider that if you are near or far-sighted."

Entering, Julien and Noah positioned themselves nearer the back pews, crowding Father Nigel.

"Mr. Preux and Mr. Satterly, you were on the cusp of being tardy. Thankfully, Ms. Bisping opted to omit the pre-lecture trivia she and I devised. You both could have missed useful information regarding your own graces," he admonished.

"It wasn't Noah's fault, sir. We would've gotten here a lot faster if I wasn't borderline delirious," swore Julien.

"He's never been to the auditorium. I couldn't just leave him stranded," Noah added, fist-bumping the elder Elehominum boy.

Their unadulterated loyalty earned Father Nigel's reverence.

"Say no more, gentlemen. Your sprouting togeth-erness is comparable to the beginnings of the broth-erhood between Rabbi Tov and I," he tittered. "We once misheard marching orders and trekked into globs of fox droppings. I could tell you tales of our shenanigans, but the smell of peppermint perfume tells me Ms. Bisping is ready to begin."

Center apron, Blair stood reincarnated. Her straw-berry blonde mane was frosted and chopped into a pixie haircut. A navy-blue sweater vest emblazoned with yellow tassels was pulled over her dress, complementary to the matching stockings she wore.

Dusting her left moccasin's buckle clean of woodchips, she readjusted to an upright poise and caught a remote that Sister Agnieszka threw, clicking its pushbutton.

"Allow me to reintroduce myself," boasted the dignified damsel, a motorized screen dropping behind her. "Born 25 December 2002, I am Blair Bisping, the latest Gelectrika to don this vest."

Energized, the visual aid displayed a palpitating electromagnetic field diagram.

"The element from which my grace comes only selects females who are conceived in a region of naturally high electrical concentrations, after lightning strikes twice. Those stringent requirements have weeded out the unqualified and infirm. Can any of you say likewise for your graces?" she queried.

Unlike Julien and Noah, Blair's overnight metamorphosis from a thuggish vagabond to a sultry highbrow did not stupefy Piper. Raised hand swishing, she was called upon.

"The Stone of Golems says us Geodactyls have a recessive gene. Bet that's why me and Mam chafe so easily."

Noah cleared his throat. "Um, there isn't a norm for Grimemories but tuns were preteen survivors of tragedies."

"You're awfully quiet," Blair noted, side-eyeing Julien. "You shared Father Nigel's wishes of me lecturing. Not forcing you to participate would be a disservice."

"Rabbi Tov considered metal a virtually indestructible grace. Can you endorse or refute his view-point?" asked Sister Agnieszka, multiplying the co-ercion.

The arm-twisting duress of being equivalently in-sightful stressed Julien. He established a worldwide reputation grounded in bottomless wit. A literal classroom leader, the inability to coherently converse about an individualized topic would discredit him.

"Envoys are trustworthy mentors but he was misinformed," Julien stated, scraping his brain for a meaningful response. "We are anointed by seven metals: lithium, titanium, copper, zinc, mercury, silver, and gold. Each melts at conflicting thermal readings, so I presume that affects the liquefaction's immedia-cy, but acute humidity withers a Goldevoire's skeletal arrangements."

Sister Agnieszka twitched at the contradiction of her slain collaborator. Noah and Piper looked at each other with open mouths, likely imagining Rab-bi Tov's opinions irrefutable. Father Nigel whistled and vacated his seat, favoring a shaded gazebo inches from the beanstalk's swirly stems.

"Your rebuttal was unpopular and arguably con-troversial, but a good segue," said Blair, transitioning to her presentation's next slide.

Nailed to a waterboard was an Asian woman whose eyelids were taped open.

Blair yawned twice. "Controlled rage is a Gelec-trika's battery but sleep deprivation diminishes our abilities, reducing 2,000 volts to a measly 30. I hope this excuses my absence at supper. Revising left me knackered so I went to bed."

"Father Nigel and I authorized your nonappearance," Sister Agnieszka responded, saluting her. "It's Mr. Preux's truancy that confuses us."

Noah elbowed Julien, who was preoccupied with observing the priest's scuttles in the gazebo.

"The Mantrametalicus has a lot of interesting info, but I got sleepy waiting for everyone to come back from stargazing in Chillingham Forest. Honestly, I don't even remember climbing into bed."

Evaluating Julien's pretext, Blair's index finger incessantly drummed on the underbelly of her chin. Squatting, she singled him out.

"Would you like to hear a parable?"

Julien's response did not matter. Blair pressed the remote's button and unveiled the concluding slide of her lecture. Draped in Viking armor, a sorority of muscular women mummified the body of their clanswoman.

"It was a stormy season in a war-torn valley. Sick and wounded, a dying warrior had frostbite. Her legs were arthritic and numb from the glacial winds," Blair narrated. "The loud tempo of nearing unicorn hooves telegraphed her rescue, she thought, but it was not her loving tribe that arrived."

The suspense of a dramatic pause allured Blair's assembly.

"Rival equestrians rounded the bend. The first one lassoed her. Then, another lashed her with a horsewhip. Finally, the tallest rider dismounted. As that obese barbarian drew closer, the restrained warrior petitioned for an honorable death."

"Oh, my days! Did those freaks get their comeuppance?" asked an indignant Piper.

"Have patience, hun," replied Blair, pacing the story. "They abducted her, venturing miles across a drying river to a swamp campsite. They beat and asphyxiated her. At dusk, they were gone. Any guesses on why she was unassisted?"

"Her sisters must've been dead as deed."

"Na, they were too busy dunchin' baddies!"

Blair debunked Noah and Piper's respective presumptions. She purported that the absent Vikings were alive, but not actively warring.

"They were asleep. Adrenaline dumps, plus the frigidness, will do that to a person," said Julien.

"Eureka," Blair cheered. "The tribe interchanged patrol schedules, which, theoretically, was an ingenious scheme to ensure they'd be well-rested. None estimated what travesties could befall their leader."

Noah nodded. "Makes sense. The moral's self-explanatory: stay woke cuz nobody is invincible."

"Tell us another," encouraged Piper, her mouth full of shells.

Observant, Julien saw Sister Agnieszka tiptoe to reunite with Father Nigel. He watched them rummage through crates underneath the darkened rooftop, muttering in whispers. The envoys' secretive actions were interesting, but Blair's lecture was not yet finished. She stroked the potted greenery that wreathed the boundaries of where she settled, evoking the Electromni's bravest fable.

"A rabbit herd was hopping contentedly through a Chinese rainforest, going about their bunny business, when two of them plunged into a ditch. All of the other bunnies gathered about to see what they could do to help their stuck chums."

"My uncle Jonty has rabbits, stinky little critters they are," Noah informed, the story's continuation censoring his chuckles.

"Seeing how deep it was, the rest of the disconcerted varmints cried and agreed that the two bunnies in the ditch should ready themselves to starve, because they were as good as dead. Refusing to accept such a hellish outcome, the bunnies began to aggressively jump. Some of the furry onlookers woefully shouted that their stunts were useless, but they were not disheartened and kept jumping," said Blair, leaping offstage.

Julien ogled her swaying hips, appreciating the sashay she employed to navigate the aisles.

"The fallen bunnies, although wracked with discomfort, jumped with oomph. Their companions yowled for them to quit. Still, both jumped harder and higher and," Blair paused, hyping the epilogue. "Gained so much air that they jounced to freedom. Astounded, the sidelined hecklers congregated and questioned how they stayed hopeful, in spite of being told their escapes were impossible. Reading their lips, the freed bunnies revealed they were deaf and the gestures made them think they were being rooted for. What the pair perceived as encouragement inspired them to keep trying."

A roar of applause cemented the tale's virtue. Soaking in the praise her storytelling produced, Blair took a bow.

"See, I pegged yi a lecturer, with your sass and spunk," lauded Noah.

"Yeah, you've got natural charisma, and it helped drive the story's message home," Julien added. "Motivational words can help someone to do the unthinkable, whereas negativity can cause their downfall. There's power in the tongue."

"Yay for disabled fur babies!"

Piper's outcry was followed by the reemergence of Father Nigel and Sister Agnieszka, who lugged a moonstone chest by its rubbery, entangled leashes.

"Kindly assemble yourselves into an alignment of last-born to eldest," the nun instructed, setting her end of that sparkly box onto the stage's crooked frontal ledge.

The Elehominum fell in, arms at their sides with erect spines. Piper and Noah occupied the first two spaces of the line. Blair was third, standing in front of Julien.

Father Nigel removed his glasses and kneeled.

"My dearest wards, you've rapidly evolved into Wolven scholars. The deathmatch with Victoria and the Oath Keepers approaches. I humbly surrender the treasures I acquired in preparation for this moment," he uttered.

Sister Agnieszka made a withdrawal from the storage housing. She placed a glistering hourglass in Father Nigel's cupped hands.

"Ms. Woolgar: the 11-year-old shaper of stones. Your courage and solemnity are hereditary. Your mother's pre-fight ritual was rubbing volcanic ashes onto her forehead. I offer you Sierra Leonean diamond smuts."

Piper tearfully accepted the donation. A Geodactyl powdered with an elusive mineral, she said, was certified worthy by an envoy's perilous crusade to procure the anointment.

Thereafter, a gunmetal canister was given to Father Nigel. Its cold edges made his dentures chatter.

"Assuredly, the prodigious adversities of boyhood have warped your psychology, but you are now our unrivaled guru of illusions. This oxygen, bottled from Mount Everest, ventilates a Grimemory's lungs. There is not a worthier possessor than you, Mr. Satterly," he exclaimed.

Outreaching, Noah collected the canister from the priest. "The Scarlet Gospels mention how enchanting the oxygen at the top of Mount Everest is. I fantasized about climbing a mountain to plant a crochet flag for those we've lost; the poles are ganna be made of Oath Keeper carcasses."

Sister Agnieszka was slower in delivering the third treasure. Bending at the waist, she presented Father Nigel with an abnormally large, chalky cranium.

"Ms. Bisping, you have written an absolution autobiography the downtrodden may find solace within. You are the spark that lights London Bridge," acclaimed the priest. "I bestow upon you the skull of the world's largest electric eel. Use it as a high-octane generator."

Hesitantly, Blair accepted what had once belonged to a majestic carnivore. Her fingers fondled the serrated teeth, currents of yellow flashes coursing through its excavated cavities.

"Coming to Edenshire has given me a roadmap to self-realization. Thanks for leading me out of the slums, away from worries of ovarian cancer recurrences, away from eventual incarceration. Should I ever forget what I've overcome, beacons of my past triumphs will become flashlights. And if my fighting underwhelms, I'll use this as a last resort," she emphatically asserted.

Simultaneously, the recipients of those extravagant gifts turned their heads to behold Julien's christening. Sister Agnieszka copied Father Nigel's submissive posture, joining him on her knees in the proposal of pure silver gauntlets that were horizontally split-bladed at the wrists.

"A boy does not exit the womb as a leader. No, he who is bound for glory will identify his ambitions, and strive to accomplish them. That, Mr. Preux, is the difference between lazy dreamers and the truest of doers," said the priest.

"You aspired to discover the peculiarities behind your great-grandfather's workmanship, and did so in spectacular fashion," the nun added.

Mirrored in the sheen, Julien did not see himself on equal footing. He philosophized that the achievements of his underlings had outshone him.

"I don't deserve these; everyone else has matured in the name of our class, not just learned their ancestral roots."

"You gave me the courage to step out of my comfort zone. I wouldn't have dared if you disagreed with Father Nigel last night," admitted Blair.

Noah juggled his canister. "Gets to be a wee bit burdensome when you're mostly surrounded by lasses who think you're a creep. I never had a brother until yi came. I'm not outnumbered anymore."

"And you showed me how to be empathetic. I didn't agree with calling your great-grandpa, but you vowed to repay the Oath Keepers for murdering Rabbi Tov, Amelia, and Abigail, even though you didn't meet them," Piper conceded.

Their back-to-back toasts lionized Julien. Vividly picturing the accounts they described, he smiled.

"Humility is a diminishing characteristic among your generation, yet it is alive and well in you," said Sister Agnieszka.

"A knighted archangel by any other name, these gauntlets, commissioned from the Vatican's storied werewolf hunters, were reserved for the coming of an exalted Goldevoire. He hath arrived," decreed Father Nigel.

Magnetism drew Julien's fingers into the netted pockets. An exact fit, the priest's prophecy had come true.

"My, my, my! Such dazzling monikers for a foursome facing death sentences. Headstones with high-falutin' epitaphs are so cute. They're a gay old time to dance on!"

Owning that gruff-pitched inflection, the lamb-masked gnome whose offbeat song incapacitated Julien swung down the grassy rafter's vegetated cables. Cloven hoofs planted in the soil, he snagged a fleeing butterfly and peeled its wings.

"You! You're that dwarf weirdo I saw before I blacked-out," Julien yelled, alarming his consorts.

"A dwarf? Oh, no, no, no. I am Agandeur Three-Chorus, Mistress Victoria's hand-picked conductor to lead her orchestra of resurrected Atlantean hobgoblins. Be respectful; I gave thee bedrest and a goodnight kiss," the intruder scoffed.

"Drugged is more like it," retorted Julien.

Spinning, Agandeur arrogantly paraded the musical weaponry strapped to his back. "Now, now, now, consider yourself lucky, mongrel. Our songs activate sedatives in our spit contrived to lull sleepless kings and queens."

"We've no interest in your faux résumé," Father Nigel scorned. "What trickery enabled you to go undetected?"

"Well, well, well, puzzled, are we? Phantom laddie has the answer. His negligent witchcraft allowed me to come in. Children shouldn't play with dead things."

Noah gasped. "The séance portal wasn't deactivated. How could I be that reckless?"

Listening and repeating, Agandeur waggled his pincers as if he was controlling a singer's rehearsal. His mockery infuriated Blair. She backhanded him, splintering that drab mask to reveal a wrinkled face riddled with gargantuan pimples and asymmetrical tusks.

Reeling, the hideous imp bared his moldy, misaligned teeth. "Temper, temper, temper. Mistress Victoria is en route and shan't be subject to impertinence!"

Violin drawn, Agandeur held the narcotic instrument under his boxed chin and primed the bow to shuffle across its ramshackle strings. A previous victim of the hobgoblin's acoustic, Julien knew the ramifications. Two or three notes would reduce them to a slumbering campground. Caution thrown to the wind, he bull-rushed the trespasser but swerved apace.

The roots of the beanstalk shot vines that hogtied and gagged Victoria's favorite flunky. An explosion of bright lights reinstated the Celortus, their gaseous bodies emitting steamy halos.

"An excommunicated nobleman cursed to brainless servitude, his rehabilitation is ours to administer. Go, the Oath Keepers are advancing the shoreline," they said unitedly.

Charm bracelets searing their wrists, Father Nigel and Sister Agnieszka looked to Julien, who practiced punching southpaw.

"I have a plan."

CHAPTER VIII

$\mathcal{M}$anhandled by strong winds, an oil tanker barreled crisscross, slashing through waters. An abomination of coppery propellers and growling engines, its hawse-holes vomited lumpy muck. The stupendous battle-ship encroached the seashore, thirty Agandeur *doppelgängers* leap-frogging overboard. Mindlessly, they stomped sand-lidded crabs in a beeline toward a purple bubble that now enveloped Edenshire Academy. Heads canted, browned solvents gushed from the nasal passages of their masks, fizzing as violins trilled a blaring song.

Straddling the bubble, Noah inhaled oxygen from the canister that was awarded to him. Bronchi purged of inflammation, his velvety lips puckered and blustered a windstorm that swirled the invaders on a carousel of blackening smolders.

"For Rabbi Tov. For Amelia. For Abigail," barked Piper, crawling onto Noah's shoulders.

A glamorous stripe incised her forehead, its glister mirroring that of the shuriken she gripped. Made from the dust of diamonds, each whetted disc was thrown with precision. She castrated the Atlantean hobgoblins, their penile hoods and swollen scrotum clinging to glitzy knives that carelessly washed away with the bloomed tide.

Noah's mandibles clamped and the horde of re-vived miscreants plummeted upended, their necks smashing. The miry overcast shadowing that slough of blood, grated neoprene, and tuning pegs evaporat-ed to expose the carnage.

"Olly olly oxen free," Noah said, popping the school's defensive encasement.

Father Nigel, wielding submachine guns, booted the backdoor open. Blasting on Julien's command, he struck the poop deck's four gasoline casks and the wheel of the boat spun aflame. Glowing blazes out-lined the bowsprit, swiftly skirting downhill. A titan-ic vigil light, the petroleum barge exploded. A stinky puff of smoke and rubble were its last rites.

A pair stood in the wake of dusty flakes. Enfold-ed in a black spandex bodysuit that was fitted with a white corset, a buxom woman took drags off a Cuban cigar. Alongside her was a mouthless, seven-foot-tall powerhouse that looked like a zombie Olympian god. His muscle-bound torso, bare and pastel blue, was layered in striations that led to an enlarged navel where maggots squirmed. The brown and red lamb-skin kilt he wore whiffled, grazing his razored knee pads.

"How cute," the vixen sneered, chucking her can-cerous stick at Father Nigel. "Some Bible-thumper and his retarded flock mean to barricade the Celortus' fortress."

Noah and Piper skied down a trail of jet-black ec-toplasm. Ahead of Blair and Sister Agnieszka, Julien skated in front of the priest to finalize the stronghold.

"This ends now. Your sideshow carnival has run its course."

"Oh, you couldn't be more correct, little boy. Our game of cat and mouse is indeed over, but whom should be an appetizer for the main entrée? You all look so tasty," said the corseted woman.

"And pray tell, Magdalene, how might a witch eat without a jaw," goaded Sister Agnieszka, whirling a bone scythe.

Spitting, the accosted trollop glowered as her name was revealed. "I've not forgotten; you bigoted nuns maimed my cousins!"

Ectoplasm earplugs withdrawn, Noah and Piper explained the women's rivalry to Julien and Blair. They said Magdalene was a fugitive, an escapee of Warsaw's calculated annihilation of witches.

"Those deviants deserved death. May the promiscuous wenches you conspired with fry," Sister Agnieszka insulted.

"That fat-nosed rabbi fried," retaliated Magdalene, her ginger fishtail braid blowing in a windswept tango. "He took a kerosene bath. I gave him a match to dry off with."

Fuming from the cold-blooded derision of their old envoy, Noah and Piper had to be constrained by Father Nigel's outstretched arms. Leery of Magdalene's pyromania, Julien was on the lookout for her arson toolbox, insensible to his deputy's festering anger.

"Chattin' mess about a man who's not here to exonerate himself," Blair said, situating her electrified headpiece in a holly shrubbery. "Come a lil' closer. I'll book you an expedited ticket to meet him, free of charge."

Sister Agnieszka cut a dividing line into the sand. "Quit while you still can. Two versus six is suicide."

"It seems I have forgotten my manners. What kind of consuls would me and Prince Calderwood be if we didn't formally introduce you to the crown jewel of the Oath Keepers?" sniggered Magdalene, sidestepping to break the barrier that concealed the third of that unholy trinity.

Tanzanite trident in her left hand, a short girl with curly gray and black pigtails nibbled on a dolphin's severed fin. Suspenders held an indigo sleeved dirndl to her small physique. Head elevating, she advertised a face full of freckles and cerulean eyes.

"Victoria," Piper hissed.

The Elehominum and their envoys observed the renegade child's plié, dying stingrays encircling her glass slippers. Disgusted, Sister Agnieszka's upper lip shuddered.

"One broiled Ashkenazi Jew, two dead kids, and a defector," satirized Magdalene, calf-length jackboots transporting her to the frontline. "I'm beginning to think you're unsuitable for this role."

Vigilant, Father Nigel was poised to let his index fingers click hot triggers, but reconsidered when Sister Agnieszka cheeped the mimicry of her covenant.

"You should have stayed in hiding. I'll pluck pickled pork from my teeth with your bones."

"The imaginary man in the sky has forsaken you. I am the way, to holocausts and lightless cities."

Prince Calderwood unfastened a nozzle from the waistline of his kilt. Thrown, it released whirls of fire that ringed Magdalene's plait and earlobes. Victoria flashed a gap-toothed grin, basking in the escalated sunlight.

"This can't be good," cautioned Julien, sweating.

"Yeah, she's somehow gotten elemental powers," Blair said.

"That woman's nothing out of the ordinary," corrected Noah. "She's a copycat sorceress. Aleister Crowley fathered plenty of weekend Satanists."

Volunteering her headdress to Piper, Sister Agnieszka confronted Magdalene. The hovering nozzle spurted a combusting octagon, neutralizing the practicalities of interference.

"The Lord's fury will be her sword and shield," Father Nigel stated, attempting to reassure his wards of the nun's hawkish competency.

Sister Agnieszka's hips widened and she swung her scythe. A bent spine denied Magdalene a beheading. Upturned palms pedaling in reverse, she spider-walked. Legs crossed, the contortionist torpedoed herself.

Drop-kicked, the envoy lurched backwards. "Devilish acrobatics won't revoke your death warrant."

Sprinting, Sister Agnieszka walloped Magdalene's ankles with the blunt half of her weapon. The sonorous thud of bone hitting bone garnered cheers from the Elehominum supporters.

"She's hurt," trumpeted Blair, mocking the nun's retreating nemesis.

A headstand redirected Magdalene. Defaulting to a bipedal foothold, she unhitched her interwoven hairpiece. It sizzled and mutated into a brimstone hatchet, lice trickling from its blade.

"Nobody's leaving this funhouse. Playtime has just begun."

The feuding women galloped to a clash. Slinking low, Magdalene swiped but Sister Agnieszka sprung high. Blowing a kiss at Blair, Magdalene snatched the hem of the nun's dress, yanking her ground-level. Sweaty foreheads bashing together, their saw-like weapons clanged against one another. A lowlife opportunist, Magdalene crunched Sister Agnieszka's nose and kneed her.

"God is our refuge and strength, an ever-present help in trouble," Piper preached, reminding her breathless envoy of their ecclesiastical convictions. "Therefore, we will not fear, though the earth give way and the alps fall into the heart of the sea, though its waters roar and foam and the skies quake with their surging."

Father Nigel piggybacked on the recital of Psalms. "The Lord is my light and my salvation. Whom shall I fear? The Lord is the citadel of my life, of whom shall I be afraid? When the treacherous advance against me to devour me, it is my enemies and my foes who will stumble and fall. Though an army besiege me, my heart will not cower. Though war break out against me, even then I will be confident."

Snickering, Magdalene reeled in a fistful of Sister Agnieszka's greasy ponytail. "Where is he, your fraudulent prophet? Blaspheme this fake God and die."

Jabbing her adversary's stomach, the nun freed herself. Revitalized, she slashed and nearly dismembered the fumbling loudmouth Oath Keeper's right arm.

Rivers of blood spurting through her ruptured synthetic fiber, Magdalene went berserk. She recklessly batted at Sister Agnieszka. One of those pendulous swings found its mark, slitting her midriff.

"If her liver's punctured, she'll bleed out," Julien said.

"She'll be the winner, she has to be," claimed Noah, hopelessly trying to sound conclusive.

"That pyromaniac will have lucked up if she is," Blair ranted. "Cuz if I get a hold of the sket, her uterus will become a battery pack."

Feminine grunts bellowed. Sister Agnieszka and Magdalene traded slices. Perspiration aggravated their wounds. Still, they combated with unyielding aggression, the noise of their stony collisions raucous and unshakable.

"You're a libertine prostitute, masquerading as a demoniac apostle," reproved the nun, hacking loose her challenger's bloodied G-string.

Magdalene back-flipped and the tips of her boots whiplashed Sister Agnieszka. Suctioned to the top of that infernal arena, she spat flaming sewage at the nun, inflicting second-degree burns to her hairline.

"That's not fair," Piper whined.

"Aww, are you panicking about dear ole Agnie," sibilated Magdalene, motioning for Piper to venture nearer. "Come to mama, I've got a pacifier you can suckle."

"My wards will not engage in any of your sinful deeds, you heathen," Father Nigel interposed.

"Testy, are we? Don't let your sexual frustrations mislead you, old man. I'll cook you faster than I did the rabbi, and these yummy kiddies will be my dessert."

The bitter verbal exchange was a useful diversion.

Like a phoenix, Sister Agnieszka rose from the cinders of chestnut hair follicles and cruddy sediments. Her hoarse screams echoed. Winding, she launched her scythe at Magdalene, cutting off three of her left fingers. Shrilling in woe, she belly-flopped.

"I've never seen something so brutal," said Julien.

"Serves that firebug right. She's gonna get hers," Blair justified.

Jiggling in a bloodbath, Magdalene endured Sister Agnieszka's high-angle stomps.

"Yes, bruise my pancreas! Great minds think alike. This is exactly what I did to that delectable Welsh girl before I flamed her. Those groans were beautiful."

Sister Agnieszka punted Magdalene, fracturing her entire top row of teeth. Drunkenly, they leaned onto each other until another forceful kick streamed them down her throat.

"Abigail had more honor in her toes than you have in the whole of your trifling body," the nun spouted. "You will rue the day you allied with the Oath Keepers."

Sister Agnieszka bounced Magdalene's head like it was a basketball, dribbling past her shaved fingers. Snatched up by her ear, she was conquered. Sister Agnieszka then stole her hatchet and threw it at the floating nozzle. The octagon of fire was extinguished.

Scythe raised, the nun readied herself to deal the deathblow when Victoria's three-pronged lance flew, harpooning Father Nigel. Trembling, he flattened to the sweltering, craggy surface.

"No, not like this," bleated Julien, rushing over to him.

Relinquishing her fine-boned pike, Sister Agnieszka scuttled to the mobbed enclosure. She pushed past the fraught children and sniveled. Cradling the priest, she remorsefully stared at the arrowheads that impaled his deltoids and gallbladder.

"I have failed."

"Don't blame yourself," Father Nigel gurgled. "It's our job to die for both, the Elehominum and the Celortus. My clock may have ticked its last tock, but I want to thank each of you for letting me be an envoy. What a wonderful life I've led."

Teary, Julien combed the priest's beard. "What kind of God lets this happen to his servants?"

"There are many unsolved mysteries of this world but to brave the unknown, to courageously fight for what's right...that, Mr. Preux, is the Wolven way," said Father Nigel, his spasms ceasing.

"He's gone," Blair whispered, shutting his eyelids.

"The reaper's come. I knew yi well," said Noah.

"Say hello to Rabbi Tov for me, please," Piper bewailed.

Enraged, Julien roared at the murderous invaders. "Piper and Noah, you take the big oaf. Blair, finish Magdalene. Victoria's mine."

Opponents allocated, the Elehominum marched to the pulse of Sister Agnieszka's sobs, the drip-drop of her liquefied gloom hitting Father Nigel's crumbled sunglasses spurring them onward.

CHAPTER IX

The dry air diminished. Refreshing breezes sailed eastward Chillingham Forest, rowing the sienna murk that overspread the residential community of Cumberchester Heights. Confined to their slummy, tumbledown cottages, the forlorn taxpayers eased their disgruntlement with crossword puzzles and scrambled television screens, clueless to the looming bloodshed.

"I won't let you harm anybody else," Julien said to Victoria.

Pivoting, he threw a hook that dislocated her jaw. Unmoved, she counted the cubical dents his silver glove left on her cheek. Pinching her jutted chin, she bumped it into place with a revolting pop.

"What the heck?" remarked Julien, backing into what felt like a cold wall of stone.

Palming his cranium, Prince Calderwood hurtled him at the burnt ship. He ricocheted off the front, immobilized in a web of heavy-knit wires and seemingly doomed to an inescapable drowning.

"And then there were three," Magdalene said, nonchalantly arising. "What will the Elehominum musketeers do now that their gutsy leader is all tied up?"

Sliding on a yellow electrical current, Blair leveled

her with a side-kick to the spleen. "Should've just slit your own damn wrists. Would have been a lot less painful than what I'm gonna do to ya."

"You must be sweet on me. Taking a bandage off hurts more than that, baby doll."

Magdalene's snide catcall antagonized Blair. Seething, she upraised her right leg and dropped it in a guillotine-like fashion, shocking the neck discs of the Oath Keepers' spokeswoman.

Julien struggled, his tangled body shimmying against the ship's gangplank. His constant squirms knocked a capstan loose. The vertical-axled machine skidded and bashed the left temple of his head. Sister Agnieszka's whimpers became indistinct. He fell unconscious, dreaming of utter decimation. He saw the Earth's seven continents submerged in a flood. World-renowned landmarks sank to an abyss of giant squid tentacles. Megalodon sharks munched frenetic swimmers, his cousin Emmanuel among them.

A saltwater wave jostled him awake. Replacing the comforting view of Blair pummeling Magdalene was Piper and Noah's luckless skirmish with Prince Calderwood. A tower of brawn, he suplexed them both at once.

"C'mon, dudes. You gotta outsmart him," Julien sleepily groaned.

On all fours, Noah blew a black tornado that fleetingly imprisoned Prince Calderwood. The brute flexed, causing the hardening ooze to fissure and ultimately disintegrate. Saw-tooth rocks in hand, Piper ran at him but was dropped with a haymaker.

Julien writhed, desperate to aid his friends. "I have to get untangled or they're gonna die."

Churning Piper's ankle counterclockwise, Prince Calderwood tortured her. A real-life banshee, she screeched, pawing sand until Victoria stepped on her fingers.

Sheathed in oily ectoplasm that took the shape of an ox, Noah bulldozed the Herculean colossus.

"Touch her again and I'll cut yi an extra pisshole," he growled, breezing Piper to safety under the shade of a walnut orchard.

Tottering, Prince Calderwood caught his balance on the wrecked vessel's foremast. Webbed feet unaffected by the stings of jellyfishes, he beat his elephantine chest and charged ahead.

"Yi must want a waltz with the underworld's favorite son," said Noah, simpering. "Let's dance, big lad."

He exhaled and windmilled an optical illusion, replicating copies of himself to confuse Prince Calderwood.

Piper sat kneading her sore joint.

"He's been trying to perfect that trick for five months now. Better late than never," she said.

The lookalike battalion surrounded the Oath Keepers' brute. Trapped, he swung impulsively but his ham hock fists passed through their ghostly visages. The one true Noah sliced Prince Calderwood, his nails tattooing abrasions on those ironclad obliques.

"Ever play skin the cat," chaffed Noah, running to add more pronounced ridges to his grisly artwork. "Too slow. Gotta be quicker than that if you're ganna stand a chance at winning, man. Yi might as well be walking on bricks!"

With one eye open, Julien, dizzied and nauseous,

watched the grating of Prince Calderwood's sides. Cut to the white meat, clotted wine-red blood squirted from his gashes. The lumbering mammoth could not apprehend Noah, who ping-ponged between imitations of himself.

An anomaly appeared in that squadron of platinum-haired boys. Pigtails swooshing, Victoria distinguished the illusionist from his fakes. She shoved him mid-dash, and Prince Calderwood punched his solar plexus. Winded, he keeled over, his conjurings fizzling.

"Noah," Piper squealed, inching upright.

Julien, sensing the urgency in her yelp, floundered toward the coastline but a tidal wave wrangled him beneath the waves. Thrashing, he fought the desperation to breathe, only to succumb to the overflow of carbon dioxide in his blood and a deficiency of oxygen. Lungs clogged, his heart hiccupped. He flatlined and hit the seabed.

"Wake up. This is not the end. It cannot be. A Goldevoire leaves no fight unfinished."

Jean-Renee's voice resuscitated Julien, algae jetting from his mouth.

"I thought I was a goner," he said, watching his great-grandfather bury clam pearls. "How are we breathing underwater?"

"Nevermind the schematics, pitit gason mwen. Your primary concern should be Noah. Prince Calderwood has discovered where his grace is concentrated, and plans to strangle him," replied Jean-Renee.

Noah's locket splashed before Julien.

"It's my fault. If I were more attentive, this would've been avoided. They'll do better without me.

I deserved to drown."

"That is not a decision for you to make, not anymore. Noah needs you. *They* need you."

Julien was refused contention with Jean-Renee's assertion. He blinked and resurfaced above the rowdy tides. The cords that arrested him, pierced by barracuda bites, deflated and cascaded into a ravine of bubbles. Edenshire Academy was a speckle in the distance. He swam, treading gunge and boating parts.

"I'm coming," called Piper, hobbling to defend her asphyxiating classmate.

Prince Calderwood throttled Noah, strangling fermented ectoplasm spittle out of him. His joggling limbs started to go limp. The vice grip that obstructed his airway suddenly unclasped.

"Get your grubby paws off him," Julien ordered, axing the stocky male with Sister Agnieszka's lost scythe.

Noah fell, breathing heavily as he saw Prince Calderwood be lacerated. Despite a hanging bladder, he was unshaken.

Headbutting the ground, Piper sent a chasm down the sand that culminated with the elevation of a wall covered in rock spikes behind Julien, who quarter-turned to the right. Charging, she used her forehead as a battering ram, her ankle buckling after contact.

Pincushioned on the prongs, Prince Calderwood was slain. Victoria, resting on a throne of dried stingrays, scowled at his crucifixion.

"I'll get you two someplace safe. Can't risk you getting hurt more," said Julien, fireman's carrying Piper and Noah.

"Just a little ice and some Nurofen, and I'll be good."

"I'm not asthmatic; give me a few seconds to catch my breath and I will cast a hex the likes of which Victoria has never seen, one that'll make her think Lucifer himself is upon us!"

Julien said he respected Piper and Noah's perseverance, but their protests were ignored. Hustling to the school's backdoor, he parked them in front of the still-crying nun.

"Sister Agnieszka, I know you're coming unglued but I need you to be strong, alright? Piper can hardly walk and Noah's wheezes are getting worse. There's no Rabbi Tov or Father Nigel to protect them. It's just you. Please, be the envoy we believe you are capable of being."

She nodded, arming herself with one of the priest's guns.

"My negligence has been a factor in all of our losses. I have dishonored every man and woman who was an envoy before me. I blame myself for the lives we've lost. I have failed again and again, and you would not be wrong to impeach me."

"We haven't lost faith in yi yet, Sister Agnieszka," said Piper.

"Nope, not even a tidbit," Noah added, his coughs harsh and gravelly. "No reason to, you're in the trenches with us."

"See, no one..."

Magdalene, cross-eyed and gasping, came shambling around the corner, interrupting Julien. Blair collared her with a nylon clothesline, kneeing her hamstrings when she tottered too far forward.

"I've whooped your ass from pillar to post, and ya haven't got a tooth to spare. I won't ask again: do you repent for the evils you've done?"

"I'm an Oath Keeper and fear no Christian gods, nor their hoodwinked worshipers. Your theological burble is meaningless."

Hearing Magdalene's venomous reply, Blair let the torturous choker drop and performed a handstand. Her thighs wrung the neck of the despicable witch. The crunchy snaps subsided, leaving her head on backwards.

"I was wondering where you were," Julien said, keeping eye contact with Blair as he massaged Piper's distended ankle. "This one and Noah could've really used some help, but it looks like you had more important engagements."

Blair wiped Magdalene's blood onto her sweater. "Never killed anybody when I ran the streets, lootin' and finessin'. Had a few knife fights and pub brawls with some punks, but none of 'em got put in caskets. I didn't think I had it in me but I was wrong. I clapped her, and won't hesitate to do the same to whoever threatens my Edenshire fam."

"You'll get that opportunity sooner rather than later. Her and Calderwood are out of the picture, but Victoria's alive," informed Julien.

"Is she? Well, no sense in makin' her wait to be reunited with her lackeys," Blair said, stepping over Magdalene.

"Raise hell on my behalf," lobbied Noah.

"We may be slower cuz of our injuries but, if you need us, just whistle," Piper stated.

Sister Agnieszka looked to Father Nigel, overwrought. "Godspeed."

Julien and Blair hugged their debilitated classmates and twitchy envoy and, in tandem, they moved to confront Victoria. Their footsteps paused at the edge of her throne.

"We don't want to do this but you are not giving us much of a choice. You should be on our side, not theirs. Don't be so foolish," implored Julien.

"Yeah, you're an Elehominum. Doesn't that mean anything to you?" Blair asked.

Snorting, Victoria sank into a puddle. She gazed upon them from a distorted world, one where fishhooks wigwagged like swing seats and albino octopuses swam, spraying their ink on overturned houses. Her honeyed lips parted as she responded bitterly.

"We are not the same."

"I'm sick and tired of these games," shouted Blair, stomping the small pool. "Ya wanna be an Oath Keeper? Fine with me. Come outta hidin' so I can show you what happens to 'em."

Her right leg glowed and she whipped it around, shattering Prince Calderwood's crucifix to splinters.

"Bee, stop. You're letting her manipulate your mood. She wants you to be a loose cannon and lose control of your grace. Victoria isn't a halfwit; everything she's doing is deliberate. It's a strategy. Don't you understand?" Julien questioned, restraining her by the wrists.

Heeding his theory, Blair calmed herself. Deep, numbered breaths conciliated her thumping heart.

She inhaled for nine seconds and then exhaled, repeating the exercise until the glisters of electricity that hooped her calves faded.

Victoria laughed, gargling oyster juices.

"You're a regular stand-up comic, huh? Welp, the joke's on you. If the Oath Keepers win, you and everyone you love are history," said Julien.

"Silence, peasant," Victoria thundered. "I'll take Elehominum lives to have me parents back, and I'll start with yours!"

Fishhooks lanced Julien and Blair's socks, towing them below the shallow waterhole.

CHAPTER X

A collaborative stench of spoiled tuna and sulfur exacerbated the bumpy slide down a long coral reef. Crashing through a blockade of mottled lobster shells, the teenagers hung over a misty canyon, strung up by the fishhooks that kidnapped them. The thin fabric of their socks unraveled and they involuntarily swooped. A mound of lily pads and sullied beach towels padded the fall.

"It's like an entire suburb sank," said Julien, looking at the assemblage of totaled cars and condominiums to the left of them.

Coasting off that hill of hodgepodges, Blair wandered, sighting a track of rumpled knickers, mops, and singed cat kennels that led to a cul-de-sac. "How have we not suffocated? The Electromni didn't say Elehominum had gills."

"Neither did the Mantrametalicus."

"You don't," confirmed Victoria, camped on a moldering house's smokestack. "But I'm a Hydrokenet, and my white blood cells release invisible tinctures that distill O2 oxygen gas."

Blair's upper lip arched in repugnance. "And ya brought us here so you'd get a homecourt advantage."

"Do not flatter yourself, you inbred hooligan,"

Victoria responded. "I wanted the two of you to have a first-hand look at what your delightful envoys neglected to tell you."

"What're you talking about?" asked Julien.

"Emily Harper was a Cumberchester Heights resident and Hydrokenet who dabbled in magic," Victoria stated, eating rotten caviar. "Townsfolk saw her walk on water to save a shipwrecked fisherman. They thought she was the Antichrist and hanged her in December of 1947. When her neck snapped, a rainstorm drowned everything. The residents tried to rebuild, but the storm kept restarting. Eventually, they gave up on its renovation but the Celortus had Edenshire Academy built here because of their guilt. They want to absolve themselves of wrongdoings by gentrifying Cumberchester Heights, yet Emily's curse is forever and someday, will swallow it whole."

"So, we're in some underwater junkyard," said Blair.

Victoria smirked. "Incorrect. Emily used her grace to sink Cumberchester Heights little by little, and made it impossible to get to this place without a Hydrokenet's help. It is now my playground."

"That's unforgivable," Julien lampooned. "You should be protecting the world, not trying to destroy it."

"Oh, I could do much more than that. Water has healing properties, and will swap the living for the dead if a Hydrokenet goes to the Bermuda Triangle with offerings of healthy hearts. I know there are two of you that will be acceptable for the revival of my parents. The leader of the Oath Keepers told me."

"Are you that stupid, Victoria? They're lyin' to you

and have been since the very start," said Blair.

"You don't remember because you were brain-washed. The Oath Keepers are the reason why your mom and dad are gone," Julien added.

"Shut your mouths! Never are you to speak ill of my deliverer," yawped Victoria, arms transforming into swordfishes that spun. "There's a new world coming and your blood will usher it in."

Jumping, she lunged at Blair, using her knees to pin her shoulders to the ground. The menacing hollers of drills deepened as they neared her jade irises. Bolting, Julien went to tackle Victoria but she spewed red-bellied piranhas that hungrily ate away his shirt. He clubbed the gluttonous scavengers, demolishing them one by one. Victoria capitalized on the deflection and sawed off the helix of his right ear. She reveled in his falsetto cries of agony, mockingly telling him to be still because Parkinson's disease ran in her family.

Glimpsing a broomstick in her peripheral vision, Blair scrabbled for it and hurried to a stand. She broke the handle over Victoria's back, stunning her.

"Gotta be something here we can patch you up with, but it'll be impossible to do so out in the open," she gauged, using Julien's wrists to pull him toward the real estate wreckage.

Musty shingles and disconnected doors were their cloaks. Shriveling high-rises jailed them, supervising a communion not meant for other ears.

"Ouch," brayed Julien.

"Lower your voice or she'll find us," Blair said, her electric fingertips cauterizing his incision. "And be happy she didn't drill your brain. No way I'd be able to doctor that."

Moping, Julien cringed at the mauled reflection a dump truck's rear-view mirror showed him. "I look like a freak."

"I think you look like a badass," argued Blair, tying him a tourniquet made of a pinstripe handkerchief and a nickel hoop.

"Really?"

"Yeah, but I'll have to disinfect your ear. You might need a tetanus shot, too. If we found this stuff just scattered about, there's probably peroxide bottles and gauze strips nearby. C'mon, let's ransack these condos."

Julien displaced the twinge of his ear, disregarding it as he inspected beeping doorbells and muddy balconies. "Okay, we can but I have a feeling Victoria booby-trapped them. The safest bets are likely the ones with unbarred windows or fire escapes, in case we need to make a quick getaway."

"BBC would sell their souls to get this scoop, fam," Blair said, following him to a section of yellow taped residences.

"And then some sleazy billionaire and his golf buddies would try to monopolize it," remarked Julien, snaking through a dog door. "Those corporate monkeys would file copyrights for asbestos poisoning, if they could."

Blair crawled in after him, invading a hedonistic hideout. Blindfold harnesses were amassed in a bathtub beside an oaken stairwell. Cast-iron paddles hung from black licorice candy straws, swaggering along the drywall ceiling.

"I really ain't feelin' this place," she mumbled, passing a wheelbarrow full of cocaine and lingerie. "It makes me remember what I heard prostitutes talkin' about in the hood."

"Well, I can see why. Do you want to try our luck elsewhere?"

Blair did not answer him. The chocolate skin of his developing back muscles hypnotized her. She counted every dimple and mole bordering the Texas-shaped birthmark above the crack of his anus. Tongue lolling, her balmy breaths became erratic and visible.

"Hey, you aren't a hypochondriac, are you?" asked Julien, turning from a rack of branding irons.

Blair cleared her throat and swallowed. "No, no. I'll be fine, just a baby migraine. Shall we go upstairs then?"

"Alright, but if you need to sit for a minute, just say so," Julien said, scaling the steps with her at his immediate left.

Attempting to ignore the silken stilettos that were superimposed on the banisters, Blair looked straight ahead. Her inner thighs sweated, cramping as they reached an incomplete bathhouse. Stoneware pipes covered the soddened floor, rattling.

"Jeez," yipped Julien, eyeballing a bed of nails beneath a sprinkler in disrepair. "Whoever lived here wasn't shy about their fetishes."

Readjusting her bra, Blair sauntered to Julien. "It's the people you least expect that'll hurt ya. You never see it comin'."

The largest pipe sprung a leak, its blowhole overflowing with hydrogen that melded in whirls to form Victoria.

"Peekaboo," she blurted, startling the Elehominum.

Blair unsuccessfully grabbed for her as she dropped into a puddle, reappearing at Julien's side. She wrenched his wrist and, in an over-the-shoulder throw, slammed him onto the grungy pipelines.

"How could either of you pretenders save the Celortus when I alone am too much for you?" denigrated Victoria, her glass slippers mashing his bandaged ear.

Blair sprinted forward with a bicycle kick, but her legs were caught and she was flung sideways, hitting a fire hydrant.

Victoria slid on a dustpan, throttling her. "Legends say the ghosts of Jack the Ripper's victims haunt this bordello. You'll be in good company after I disembowel you."

"I'm afraid that's where you're wrong, Vickie," Julien said, refocusing her scrutiny to his recovery. "She won't be pushing up daisies anytime soon, not on my watch."

Blair exploited the distraction. Gouging Victoria's eyes, she thrust her toward a silvery punch that caved her snub nose in with the velocity of a World Series-winning pitch. Intuiting victory, the Elehominum swarmed her with high to low blows.

"And to think I almost felt sorry for you," bayed Blair, her electric kicks welting Victoria's chicken legs.

Victoria's head bobbled from Julien's jabs, the clang of metal tenderizing facial meat and bone clamorous.

She withstood their double-team incursion, acting only when they fatigued.

"You've worn yourselves out. The time has come for your final rests," Victoria said, sweeping Blair's legs from under her.

Kicking Julien in the penis, Victoria sent him to his knees. She peppered him with punches and elbows that were intended to cause a concussion.

"You won't win," he burbled.

"I already have," replied Victoria, her anemic knuckles splitting Julien's upper lip.

Dizzy, Blair stumbled to her feet and clumsily ran back into battle.

"You've lost," Victoria vilified, her fingertips discharging a swirling stream that washed the incoming heroine dangerously close to the bed of nails. "Surrender to the waves, just as Amelia did!"

Blair splashed, fighting the increasingly violent current of that hydrous merry-go-round. Julien, battered and punch-drunk, watched the swiveling waters rise to her cheeks.

"No," he droned, onlooking as the chancellor of the Oath Keepers pursued his defenseless classmate.

Victoria's hands mimicked those of a piano player, masterfully pressing invisible keys that orchestrated a full-blown whirlpool. Obsessed with swamping Blair, she was incognizant of Julien's creeping advances. Shouldering a 12-inch bolt cutter, he bludgeoned her, bending the cudgel's resistant handles.

Cerebellum hemorrhaging, Victoria hobbled and underwent a seizure.

"Grab me," Julien said, reaching for Blair.

Latching onto his arm, she was wrested to freedom.

"Has she croaked?" asked Blair, burping up plankton. "I could barely hear, let alone see, in that murky water."

"Not yet," Julien presaged, letting go of the bloody tool he held.

Victoria quaked, unable to postpone the reversion of her hands to swordfishes.

Julien balked as she urinated on herself, the involuntary runnel yellowing her white shoestrings. Clearheaded, he saw her for what she truly was: a sick, misguided little girl.

"I'm sorry," he atoned, uppercutting Victoria.

She backstroked through the muggy air, pancaking onto the nail bed. Her mouth slavered a final foamy spillover and the twitches remitted.

The teenagers were stock-still in disbelief, listening to the hot pipes tweet steam over Victoria's body.

"You did it, you really did it," rejoiced Blair.

Slumping, Julien eased his head onto her exposed shoulder. "Correction: we did it."

"Don't get too comfy, cameraman," Blair said, tightening the knot that kept his ear insulated. "I ain't your mummy; don't be expectin' me to breastfeed ya."

"Ha, you're so hilarious but I'm lactose intolerant. Try again, Ms. Impractical Joker."

Blair squinted, noticing that dusky floodwater had begun to funnel through the expanse's underpinnings. "Unless you've got a sadistic sense of humor, you won't think what's coming next is too funny."

A blowout of water sloshed upstairs, bowling them to the fabled whorehouse's first-floor.

"We were only able to be here because of Victoria. It's re-locking itself now. We have to get to that opening before it closes," apprised Julien, the ebb and flow pushing him out the doorway.

Submerging herself, Blair jetted after him.

They swam for what they thought was a millennium, watching their escape route's unceasing shrinkage as they bypassed an octopus' clutches.

Reuniting with the fishhooks that were deployed as abductors, Julien and Blair climbed the barbed canes, earning breaths of fresh air. Wheezing, they evacuated the puddle and sat seaside, their backs to the crinkling waves.

Piper shambled off a gurney, cheering their victorious return. "And the Lord delivers them, just as he did Daniel!"

"Father Nigel has been avenged," said Noah.

Crying, Sister Agnieszka gave them a standing ovation.

"No one's going to believe some kids saved the Earth, but there's no way I'm not telling my grandchildren about what happened these past few days," laughed Julien.

"You have saved nothing," Victoria disputed, rising from the watercourse with alligator tails filling her punctures.

CHAPTER XI

Victoria's reptilian extensions eclipsed the sun. Ruffling, they turned turquoise, and disgorged wastewater jets that hosed Julien and Blair toward their sour-faced companions. Independently, the trident that gored Father Nigel ejected from his wounds and cruised back to her, slanting before her lips.

"I pray she does not do what I suspect," Sister Agnieszka confided.

The Elehominum saw their envoy's neck hairs rise, her tone defeatist. Jittery, she aimed both of Father Nigel's submachine guns but did not speak.

"Do what? What else is there that you haven't told us?" chided Julien.

Preferring to act instead of clarifying, Sister Agnieszka sniped at Victoria. She emptied the two 100-round drums. A grainy waterfall guarded her target, blocking the bullets.

Blair stepped in front of the nun. "He asked you a question."

"She descends from a Celtic family that worshiped Leviathan," divulged Sister Agnieszka. "Rabbi Tov told me that was why the Oath Keepers chose her. She can summon the Great Beast."

"Leviathan?" Julien and Blair parroted, ignorant.

Piper shivered. "Some say it's a hydra. Others, a serpent. Whatever it is, the Bible tells us it cannot be tied down, nor tamed."

"I don't consider myself to be much of a Christian theologian but the descriptions, if I remember them correctly, sounded like a Kronosaurus," said Noah. "Regardless, we have to find a way to prevent her from summoning it."

Victoria demanded their attention, her palms thunderously clasping the trident.

"She must be stopped," Sister Agnieszka enjoined, prompting Blair to fetch the electric eel skull gifted to her.

Distrusting of the nun's mental state, Julien evaluated the wellness of Piper and Noah. They were welted and dog-tired, yet unafraid to die.

"It's now or never," stated Blair.

"I don't care what happens; you all have become the clique I never expected to be a part of," Julien confessed, returning Noah's locket. "Let's finish her."

The five of them scampered, intending to interrupt Victoria's sacrilegious conjuration. Aching and sluggish, they were unsuccessful.

"Usurper of ten thousand oceans. Black-hearted undertaker. Hope's destroyer. I offer you the blood of an envoy and an entire settlement to ingest. Arise from your hibernation beyond the coastline. Claim the treasures of this world as your own. Awake, Leviathan!" intoned Victoria.

Fastening her mouth to a headjoint the trident sprouted, Victoria blew a chord that simmered the waters as an inordinate shadow incarnated. An obscenity of draconic scales and green-gray hide, a croc-odile the size of a humpback whale arose, consuming the hulled oil tanker in one fell swoop.

"Dear Lord, the dragon of end times is upon us," Sister Agnieszka gasped, peering into its beady eyes.

Hoisting its girthy, axe-shaped tail, Leviathan launched a fireball that sautéed a quarter of Cum-berchester Heights. Blythe Gardens, a daycare, and a row of foreclosed diners were reduced to crispy crumbs.

"And now the plague commences," forewarned Victoria, lifted onto the behemoth's snout by its brin-dled tongue. "Those unsuited for the reborn world must be expunged. Run while you can, or be killed now like the pigs you are."

Noah blew vapory needles at Leviathan. Inhaling each, it breathed a smokescreen that chloroformed him. Scurrying to his aid, Sister Agnieszka went to scoop the comatose boy up, but was putted over the horizon and into the bubbling depths by the aquatic predator's tail.

Methodically rubbing the last bit of diamond dust between her hands, Piper engineered a glistening shield that temporarily hid them from view.

"We need to get to Wuthering Lake. There's poaching equipment that Rabbi Tov never threw away after he caught some traveling ivory hunters. Their leftover nets and grenades might help," she said, trying to shake Noah conscious.

"Yeah, and there may even be bear mace or a har-poon," added Blair.

Looking to the reservoir that neighbored Chill-ingham Forest, Julien estimated the distance they would have to run. "It's far but we can make it. I'll carry Noah. On my mark, I want everyone to sprint. One. Two. Thre..."

Disrupting the countdown, Leviathan's claws decimated their shield. The smackdown impact drove the Elehominum apart, pairing them off.

"United you stand, divided you fall," Victoria decried, watching Piper and Noah barrel roll to Edenshire Academy's storm cellar. "Hideaway, piggies. We will take you to the slaughterhouse, too, once the meatier swine has been sent through the scalding tanks."

The genocidal titan she summoned gave chase to Julien and Blair, trailing their tumbles into the tranquil woodland. Its tail swished, sawing down trees.

Hidden inside a cornfield marsh, they communicated through whispers.

"How are we supposed to fight that? It could probably eat the school, and have room for what's left of Cumberchester Heights," said Blair, grimacing as Leviathan squished squirrels.

"Bee, if I had an answer for that, we wouldn't be sitting ducks," Julien responded. "Should've asked Piper or Sister Agnieszka what the Bible says can overcome it. I'm sure they'd know."

Blair lowered her head. "Sister Agnieszka, she's…"

"Hey, I'm sure she's alive," Julien lied, combing her crinkly hair. "We'll rescue her. I promise."

The squawk of Edenshire Academy's watchful peregrine falcon beckoned them to look to the evening sky. Whizzing through the underbrush, she parachuted a metallic bow and arrow.

"I think I know how we can kill it but if I'm wrong,

we're toast," counseled Julien, softly disseminating the instructions.

Leviathan's roars resounded, sonic booming the windows of any nearby building it had not cremated during its calamitous manhunt. The plant life its bristly underbody touched wilted instantaneously.

"I expected so much more of you two, but you've disappointed me by hiding here. Where will you cower when it's slurped dry?" Victoria upbraided, voyaging on the monstrous vertebrate's horny plates.

A human candlelight, Blair balanced on a log. She was helmeted by the electric eel skull. Vermilion sparks gathered about her head, steadily brightening. Behind her, Julien unwrapped his disjointed ear and clawed it, bleeding 12 drops onto the bow and arrow.

"There's something I've been wanting to say to you."

Incensed at the very peep of the Gelectrika's voice, Leviathan stampeded, its triangular, plaque-slathered teeth smoking.

Blair ducked and Julien slingshotted a golden broadhead arrow. "Take your new world and shove it."

Neck whipping, Blair saturated the projectile with lightning bolts. Coiling, it penetrated Leviathan's endoskeleton, ricocheting off the stout bones. Continually electrocuted, the hellspawn went shambling backward. It fell, crushing Victoria beneath its blundering form. When the wriggles and throaty growls stopped, the once bloodthirsty carnivore was memorialized in 24 karats of taxidermy.

"Guess that put a stop to whatever bizarro utopia they imagined having. Would've been nice if we could have caused a breakthrough, though," said Julien.

Blair removed her helmet. "Lil' scallywag was probably a fan of Hitler and his Nazi eugenics shtick. She and that oversized lizard got what was comin' to them."

"Have a heart, Bee."

"A heart? She took our envoys from us, Julien. Father Nigel needs a coroner. Sister Agnieszka might be somewhere concussed. Excuse me, but screw her *and* her dead parents!"

"You're right. I...just wish we could have gotten to her sooner. You know, before the kidnapping. She didn't even get to be a teenager. She was barely older than Piper."

A bouquet of ironweeds, withering and half-eaten, streamlined between Julien's legs. He yanked them by the plastic bag that packaged them together, slogging past Blair.

"My mom taught me that no one is inherently bad," he said, laying the wildflowers before Victoria's dislodged slippers. "Most people, good or evil, get to make their own choices. Hers were made for her. She didn't have a chance."

Joining him at the foot of that gold-crested carcass, Blair held his hand. "And we made our choices to protect the Earth. It had to be done."

"I know. You can't save everyone but some die too late and others, too soon," Julien mourned.

"There's nothin' else to do. You've paid your respects. Let's find Noah and Piper," advocated Blair, pulling him away.

They plodded through the guck of mushy mud, tidewater, and steamrolled rodents. Julien obsessively peeked over his shoulders, secretly hoping that Victoria would rise and thank them for showing her the error of her ways. She remained incarcerated underneath the juggernaut that crushed her, lifeless. An eastern breeze whisked her slippers further into the bog, where they slowly sank to the bottom.

Limping, Piper and Noah met them at the seafront. Intending to use the resurfacing sun to their offensive advantage, they reorganized back-to-back.

"How're you guys doin'? Any sprains or bruises?" solicited Blair.

"I'm in tiptop condition, and ready to blow Victoria straight to Orion's Belt," Noah yapped, nostrils flaring.

Piper clapped, fluorescent dust falling off her calluses. "Wey aye, she and her scaly pet won't withstand the wrath of diamond miners!"

"She's dead. Leviathan, too," informed Julien.

"If I didn't have to give Noah CPR, I would've been there to see it for myself," Piper said, pouting. "How'd you do it?"

"The bird dropped what Rabbi Tov told you she was guarding. It was a bow and arrow made of holmium," explained Julien, toting the weapon. "That eel skull charged Blair's grace. I used her high voltage to transmute the arrow into gold with drops of my blood. I shot it, and she powered it with lightning blasts that electrocuted them both. Leviathan accidentally smushed Victoria when it fell."

Noah raised his fist. "I suppose that's why your ear is in shambles. Props for making that bodily sacrifice. You literally left a piece of yourself on the battlefield to save the Earth. Cheers, mate."

"We all did, not just me. Everyone sacrificed a piece of themselves to win this fight," Julien stated, raising his fist alongside Blair and Piper.

"So, what are we ganna do now?"

Piper's question picked at Julien's brain. As the unquestionable leader of the Elehominum, he had to decide what came next: assisting in the assumed Cumberchester Heights relief efforts or finding Sister Agnieszka. He peered at Father Nigel's body, and discarded his gloves and the bow.

"We'll prepare his funeral arrangements. I won't have him being food for the rats; he isn't roadkill. Help me get him inside, please."

A flashbang grenade rolled out of the school's open backdoor, detonating a blinding searchlight that halted the children's progress. Disoriented, they were easy targets. Twenty troopers, uniformed in subdued urban digital camouflage and Hungarian M67 gas masks, had ambushed them. Their laser-point shotguns cocked.

"Envoy Monarchical Court Commandos! Noah Satterly, Piper Woolgar, Blair Bisping, and Julien Preux, you are hereby under arrest for a direct violation of penal code 460.00: the murder of a fellow Elehominum," the shortest officer announced.

"No, you've got the facts misconstrued," rebutted Julien, witnessing the handcuffing of his classmates. "Victoria almost destroyed our planet."

Hearing the beeps of a deep submergence subma-

rine, the officer gun-butted Julien.
"Load them on."

Acknowledgements

I would like to thank:

Neshelle Cortez, Nevelious Jordan Sr.,
Johnetter Nelson, Nijuan Jordan, Treveta Smith,
Yolanda Jordan, Jacob Proctor, Charles Cortez,
The Carthens, The Upshaws, Maurice Primrose III,
Arrie Hurd, Reginald Denney, Russell Harris,
Joshua Grant, Maurice Butler, Debra Chemotti,
and Angela Tvarozek.

A Conversation with Nevelious Jordan

Nevelious Jordan is a graduate of Virginia Commonwealth University. His debut novel, *School of the Wolven Way*, is the first title to be published by Shatteringham Books. He recently sat down with the company's creative director, Edward Huffington, to discuss his path to becoming an author.

What made you want to become an author?

I have always dreamed of writing my own books, but feared them being trashed by critics. When I turned 26, I reached a point in my life where I no longer cared about anyone's approval and decided it was time.

Have any particular authors influenced you?

Certainly. Growing up, I was a massive fan of R.L. Stine. My favorite author of all-time, though, is Ransom Riggs. The Miss Peregrine's Peculiar Children series restored my interest in recreational reading after college.

How did you come up with the idea for School of the Wolven Way?

Once I knew for sure that I would write a novel, I came up with the characters. It was very important for me to have characters that weren't carbon copies of other popular YA characters. Julien is a black teenager, which isn't typical of the lead characters in the YA books that I have read. Piper has skin and hair conditions. Noah modified his face in one of the sickest ways imaginable to cope with his troubles. He also uses ectoplasm, which is totally creepy and unique because it is a supernatural gas. Blair is a cancer survivor and despite being a cute little blonde, is tough as nails with a hustler's mentality. I tried to make each of them different because I thought it would make them learning to work together a fun read.

Regarding the setting, why did you choose Newcastle upon Tyne?
There is no place on Earth that means more to me than Newcastle. My heart is there. It is the most beautiful place I've ever seen, and I'm terrified of anything ever happening to change that.

What, if anything, inspired the concept of Cumberchester Heights?
Being that I have never seen a place in Newcastle that I find to be ugly, I wanted to create one for the story. I sat for about an hour, thinking about what makes an area undesirable. I didn't want to use the stereotypical elements of a ghetto. I wanted to create an environment where people would literally be dwelling in a living hell. I also wrote a poem from the perspective of a Cumberchester Heights resident. I'm told it'll be featured right after this interview.

Now that you have written your first novel, what is next?
Well, I plan on starting the sequel in the next few months. If we are talking long-term, though, I would

love for this book to be turned into a movie one day.

If you could cast anyone you wanted and they could pull off the accents, who would you pick?
I'd choose Daniel Kaluuya from 15 years ago to play Julien. Brianna Hildebrand would be Blair. Pixie Davies, in my opinion, would be the best choice for Piper. Brenock O' Connor would make an excellent Noah. Tobin Bell has the talent to really bring Father Nigel to life on the big screen. I think it would be cool to see Anneliese van der Pol in a serious role as Sister Agnieszka. Isabelle Fuhrman played one of the creepiest kids I've ever seen in *Orphan*, so she (at that age) would be a natural fit for Victoria. That's all I can think of off the top of my head.

Can you tell us anything about the sequel?
Sure, but I won't give away too much. It'll be longer than *School of the Wolven Way*, a new Elehominum will be introduced, and the book will pick up exactly where this story left off.

Turn Back, Kind Stranger

Please, give
Cream of wheat for the poor to eat
Blankets and toasties for the children who live in or-
phanages without heat

Sing us a carol
It has been so very long since anyone sung
Now, everyone sleeps, waking only to sip from their
wine barrel
The last I remember was when the town heretic got
hung

Oh, kind stranger
Won't you stay awhile
And shield us from danger
No, you'll just leave cold footprints on our tile
Because you don't have to endure the fistfights

We share no camaraderie
You never walked home, in darkness, on sub-zero
temperature nights
We differ, mentally and bodily

Don't prolong your stay
Go, follow the busted street lights
We don't want to hear the lies you say
You do not belong in Cumberchester Heights

Glossary of Terms

Aye　　　　British equivalent of the word
　　　　　　"yeah," used as slang

Bruv　　　　British equivalent of the word
　　　　　　"bruh," used as slang

Brummie　　An individual/dialect from
　　　　　　Birmingham, England

Celortus　　The embodied consciousness of
　　　　　　elements

Chum　　　British equivalent of the word
　　　　　　"friend," used as slang

Daft　　　　British equivalent of the word "silly,"
　　　　　　used as slang

Doon　　　A Geordie pronunciation of the
　　　　　　word "down"

Divvent fash yisel　A Geordie phrase that
　　　　　　means "Don't worry yourself"

Elehominum　Individuals empowered by the
　　　　　　elements

Electromni　A governing scroll given to a
　　　　　　Gelectrika

Geet walla　A Geordie expression that means "a
　　　　　　large amount"

Gelectrika　An Elehominum with the powers of
　　　　　　electricity

Geodactyl　An Elehominum with the powers of
　　　　　　terra firma (earth)

Geordie　　An individual/dialect from Tyneside,
　　　　　　an area in northeastern England

Goldevoire　An Elehominum with the powers of

metal

Grace   Elemental power

Grimemory   An Elehominum with the powers of ectoplasm

Howay   A Geordie expression that is generally used as a cry of encouragement

Hydrokenet   An Elehominum with the powers of water

Innit   British contraction of the phrase "Isn't it"

M'swete'w tout bon bagay
      Translated, this phrase means "I wish you the best"

M'ap fe tout efo pou mwen apran
      Translated, this phrase means "I'll do my best to learn"

Mantrametalicus A governing book given to a Goldevoire

Mavkardia   The evil descendants of the rogue element (darkness)

Neet   A Geordie pronunciation of the word "night"

Numpty   British equivalent of the word "stupid," used as slang

Pitit gason mwen   Haitian Creole for "my great-grandson"

Popped clogs   British phrase that means a person has died

Proper canny A Geordie expression that means "really good"

Reet   A Geordie pronunciation of the

	word "right"
Sket	British insult that means "slut"
Synthetarian	An Elehominum with the powers of verdure (vegetation)
Yampy	A Midlands word that can mean an individual is silly

www.ingramcontent.com/pod-product-compliance
Lightning Source LLC
Chambersburg PA
CBHW032012170626
46807CB00006B/2766